PRAISE FOR **LUCK**

"The dynamic of this group is both complicated and instantly readable in the way the characters interact with each other, and that clarity is a compliment to Constantine, who has a keen sense of the way individuals play off each other."

—ALA Rainbow Roundtable

PRAISE FOR **OLYMPIA KNIFE**

Finalist, 2017 Foreword INDIES Book of the Year | LGBT & Literary

"[STARRED REVIEW]… Americans don't have fairy tales: we have legends. Tall tales. [The world of *Olympia Knife*] is vibrant, dangerous, and a smart commentary on social prejudices against outsiders. Queer, differently-abled, fat, and nonwhite characters pack the pages. Set in the postbellum South, *Olympia Knife* is, at its core, a story about a culture that is no longer able to ignore its own diversity or the itch for change. Author Alysia Constantine is a superb writer whose distinctive, rich style makes *Olympia Knife* a pleasure from beginning to end."

—*Foreword Reviews*

"FOUR STARS… The world of *Olympia Knife* is one that goes beyond genre definitions and expectations. It's a deft historical fantasy romance that addresses issues of queerness and marginalization through the lens of a tight-knit traveling circus. Constantine's writing is evocative; it reads like a tale being told over a crackling campfire… [*Olympia Knife* is] a gentle historical fantasy with a hint of magic, perfect for readers who love queer romances and books such as *Tipping the Velvet* or *Water For Elephants*."

—*RT Book Reviews*

PRAISE FOR **SWEET**

"[STARRED REVIEW]… all romance, endlessly surprising, and nothing like any genre offering this season."

"FOUR STARS… The narrative quality is unique. Readers who are looking for a new way to tell a romance story will really enjoy how the narrator breaks the fourth wall and speaks directly to them… If you are looking for a sugary read with a dash of pain and healing, pick this one up. Once you get into it, you'll find yourself unable to stop."

LUCKMONKEY

ALYSIA CONSTANTINE

interlude press

Published by Interlude Press
an imprint of Chicago Review Press, Incorporated
814 North Franklin Street
Chicago, IL 60610

The learning process is something you can incite, literally incite, like a riot.

—Audre Lorde, *Sister Outsider*

CONTENT WARNINGS

To paraphrase author Adam Sass, this novel may contain instances of queer pain but is not *about* queer pain. It is an attempt to reflect honestly the experiences many in our queer/trans community know well: deliberate misgendering, homophobic/transphobic language, financial insecurity, food insecurity, houselessness, self-harm and reckless acts.

I probably don't need to warn for fierce loyalty, love, self-discovery, found family, creativity and joy, but those are here, too.

CHAPTER 1

THE COST OF EVERYTHING

Dear homeowner:

Congratulations! Your possession has been Uprooted.

Do not be alarmed: you have not been robbed, nothing has been damaged, and no one has been harmed; your ___TV___ has simply been repossessed by the universe. Since it was made of atoms that move freely and belong to no one, it was never yours to begin with, but only appeared temporarily to be in your home. It could have stood anywhere, had the atoms collected in another place instead of there. Do not mourn its loss, for it is not gone; rather, it has been absorbed into the Great Exchange.

To compensate for the loss you probably feel, the universe has left you this very nice ___set of golf clubs___. Please enjoy!

—The Uproots

T HAD BEEN OUTVOTED BY the others when T wanted to call the band Public Disturbance. Instead, the band became The Dispossessed because Peebo suggested it and everyone thought it was funny and a sly in-joke, given their secret relieving-people-of-their-possessions project. Peebo, being the only one among them who could draw a little and write legibly, had been put to the task of designing a logo to go with the new name, something that captured the facts that the band's music was politically charged and that it was a serious band that made real music. Vas wanted the logo to show also that the band was strictly anti-racism and anti-violence so nobody would confuse them with Nazi skinheads or something, and Kohl wanted it to somehow capture what the band sounded like. T insisted that the logo not be too accessible, in order to ward off image-conscious mall-punk poseurs, but Peebo wasn't quite up to the task and wound up handing over a crappy scribble of a kangaroo kicking the air and wearing a T-shirt with the band's name on it. Everybody had agreed that it was pretty bad. Kohl pointed out that the kangaroo might make people expect them to be Australian, but nobody could do any better, so the logo stayed. T just hoped people wouldn't start calling the band The Mates or The Aussies or something equally sad.

The band had wanted to live together, somewhere without too much negative impact, somewhere they could sleep and eat and practice loudly and not put more coin in some rich asshole's pockets. Nobody could agree on a good place, so they all gave up and crashed together in a burned-out building near Pitt campus. Kohl and T had scrubbed the soot off the walls and tried to air it out so it didn't smell so much like burned toast and had stolen enough milk crates from the back of the supermarket to make all kinds of pretty good furniture (stacked up for storage, or piled with a bunch of coats and blankets on top for sitting); everyone felt pretty good about the spiffing-up efforts until Peebo called them sellouts.

"I just got sick of smelling burned stuff and sitting on a dirty floor," Kohl said. She was tying about half of her black hair into a stringy mess on top of her head so she could shave off the rest of it.

"Lame," Peebo said. "You can still smell burned stuff anyway, and all you got out of it was an entire day of scrubbing the walls like a suburban housewife. There were probably better ways you could use your time." He sat heavily on the pile of coats and milk crates and kicked his feet up.

2

"Smug asshole," T said. "We worked all day. And Kohl has *homework*. And you're sitting there enjoying the fruits of our labor."

"Suckers," Peebo said.

"Asshole," T repeated, and Kohl nodded until Peebo snorted and flipped the chunk of bleached hair above his eyebrows. (It was the only hair left on his head, since he'd shaved the rest, but there remained a black, stubbly band on his scalp surrounding a bare, probably bald, spot that made him look like a punk monk.)

Peebo flipped the blond wisp and said, "Yep, that's right," then leaned back into the coats to take a nap. He was so string-beany that, when he lay back, he disappeared into the coats until he vanished almost completely from view, except for his long, javelin legs dangling off the end of the crates.

Kohl threw a shoe clear across the room so it bounced off the wall above Peebo's knees, but Peebo didn't move, only snorted and chuckled softly. Kohl shoved a stack of books and papers into a plastic shopping bag and heaved it over her shoulder.

"Right," she said and slammed out of the place with the blue smiley face on the bag bouncing against her back as she went. *Come Again!* the lettering read. The bag flopped as if waving goodbye. She left a revolting pile of limp hair on the counter with the utility knife smacked down on top of it like a statement.

"You didn't have to do that," T told Peebo, clicking Kohl's blade back into its handle and sweeping the wisps of hair into a piece of newspaper. "Isn't it enough that we cleaned the place for you? You have to make her feel bad about it too?"

"I didn't ask you to clean it up; that was *your* choice," Peebo said, not even opening his eyes. "Not my fault she's all tender and sensitive."

It's like talking to a rubber wall, T thought. If T punched Peebo, T's fist would only bounce back, causing damage to T's own face, while Peebo would persist un-punched in his smug contentedness. *Rubber and glue*, T thought. *Fuckyoufuckyoufuckyou.*

3

WHEN VAS CAME HOME FROM his Legitimate Job selling printer ink and ballpoint pens and reams of bleached paper to office managers and college kids, Peebo was still asleep on the crates, and T and Kohl were cooking rice and something vaguely green and sulfurous over a fire they'd lit in the sink. Vas threw his backpack on the floor next to the front door and kicked off his oxfords without untying the laces.

"Smells disgusting. What is that?" he asked.

"Curried cabbage and carrots," T said. "You're going to wreck those shoes."

It wasn't a very good or sophisticated curry, since all they could really afford was a jar of off-brand curry powder and some salt, but it was yellow and smelled spicy and did, mostly, the trick.

Vas said, "Looks like baby food. Smells like baby sh—"

"Here you go," Kohl interrupted and lumped a heap of the stuff in a bowl, sliding it onto the kitchen counter. She raised her eyebrows at Vas.

"I'm not eating that mess," Vas said, unclipping his tie and nametag. He threw them on the ground next to his backpack. "I'm the only one who has a real job around here. I should get to say what we eat."

"Eight-dollar-an-hour power," T mumbled.

"I want man food, not baby food. You don't even need teeth for that," Vas said.

"If you want a say, you should cook once in a while," Kohl said. "And stop acting like a baby if you don't want baby food. Plus, T works at the laundromat, and Peebo sells stuff in front of Pitt, and extra plus, my school *is* work, you bimbo, even if it doesn't pay."

"Yet," T said, and smooched Kohl on the forehead.

"Right. The lit major's going to make us all rich," Vas snarked. He nodded disdainfully at the green mess. "That smells like somebody beefed."

"Somebody Beefed: It's What's for Dinner," T mumbled like the Voice-Over Guy from the commercial.

Vas kicked a blue, already-busted milk crate clean across the room. "T, man, shut *up*!"

"Don't call me 'man,'" T said.

Kohl said, "That's pretty nasty, even for you, Vas."

"I wasn't—" Vas said, then stopped. "You know what? I don't even care to explain it to the two of you nimrods. I'm tired. From *working*. For *money*. You all should try it once in a while. I'm sick of being the breadwinner here."

Kohl sighed. "Oh, *bread*."

"I remember bread," T said fondly.

At that, Vas stomped across the room and yanked the blanket-curtain closed over the sleeping bag he'd spread on the floor. The blanket made a mild *whisk-flump* sound; it wasn't a satisfying statement, apparently, because, from inside the fort, T heard him punch the plaster wall, then grumble, "Shit. Ow."

"Vasilakis, you suck!" Kohl yelled in his direction. Then she put a hand on T's shoulder and squeezed. "You okay?" she asked quietly.

"Used to it," T said. "What's new? It's fine."

"It's not okay, what Vas said." Kohl laid her cheek against T's arm. "If you don't want to be a man, you don't have to be."

"I'm not. It's got nothing to do with wanting."

"That's not what I meant," she said, reaching up to brush T's curls aside. T was the only one among them with a really good, full head of hair, and sometimes it seemed as though Kohl coveted it, even though she shaved her own head—at least the bottom part—and seemed proud enough of the polished skin of her skull to shine it up with wax pretty regularly. "I meant it should be your choice, is all."

"It's not my *choice*," T said. "It's just how it *is*."

"It could be your choice," Kohl said.

"Maybe for someone else. Not me. And even if I wanted a choice, it's not like most people would let me have one."

"Fine, I tried. You don't have to be so militant, you know, I'm on your side." Kohl sighed heavily and went back to stirring the horrible

5

green crap, then dumped the entire pot of cooked rice into it. It made a sticky, puke-green mess. She tasted it, then shook her head.

"S'bad," she said.

"Yeah," T said without tasting it. "It's pretty bad."

ONCE IT HAD GONE DARK and Peebo had woken up, the four of them took Peebo's junker into Squirrel Hill. They parked by a building and hauled the huge, nearly new TV out of the flatbed, carrying it right past the doorman and into the elevator. They rode to the top floor, where Peebo jiggled every doorknob until he found one unlocked, and they snuck into the apartment.

The place was unlit, except for the ambient moonlight filtering through the uncurtained windows. There were doilies on everything, and a giant painting that seemed to be an entire canvas of navy blue hung on one wall.

"They're so rich, there's not even streetlights or traffic noise in here," Kohl marveled.

"A rich guy is standing on the street when a car sideswipes his Porsche and rips the door off. He's furious about his car. When the cops get there, he bitches, and the cop says, 'You're so upset about your car, you didn't even notice your arm's ripped off!'" T said.

"That's gross," Kohl said. "That didn't happen!"

"No, it's a joke, you have to wait for the finish," T said. "The cops say, 'Your left arm's ripped off and you didn't even notice!' And the guy looks at the bloody stump, and it's spurting blood, like, *psh psh psh*—"

"This is getting really gross. Get to the point."

"He looks at his bloody stump and says, 'Oh my god, my Rolex is gone!'"

"Look at all this ridiculous crap," Peebo said, ignoring them. "This guy would make Robin Leach jealous. Good thing we're here."

"Preach," Vas said, and everybody looked at him as if he'd just busted out in song.

"What?"

"Really?" Kohl said, as though it wasn't even a question.

T could barely see anything in the dark but could just make out the dim shapes of two overstuffed chairs, a polished table, and a swan-like floor lamp.

"Smells like a closet," T said.

"It's these yuppie wood chips." Peebo knocked over a bowl of shavings on a table by the door. "It feels like *American Psycho* or something in here."

"Hurry before Patrick Bateman gets home," T whispered.

"Those aren't wood chips, you ass, it's potpourri," Kohl said.

"It's still rich people crap. Peebo's right," Vas hissed. "Rich people pay some maid to sweep this stuff out of their house, then turn around and pay more to buy a plastic bag of it at the Overpriced Crap for Dicks kiosk at the mall and put it in a fancy dish to make their house smell like a hamster cage."

"I guess you would know better than any of us," T muttered.

Vas's face went red, and his nostrils flared. "I live in the same crap den you do."

"For now," T said.

"What's that supposed to mean?" Vas said. He stood taller and somehow looked more puffed-out than usual.

"Fight!" Peebo said. He looked as if he was going to chant.

Kohl rolled her eyes. "Leave it. We don't have time."

They lugged the television to the center of the room and cracked it down on top of the shining, curvy-legged table by the chairs.

"Let's take the rug," Peebo said.

"Too cumbersome," T said.

"There's nothing else here anyone could *use*," Peebo said.

"This, then." Kohl smacked her hand on the back of one of the overstuffed chairs. "It's probably worth about the same."

"It's part of a set, though," Vas said. "Shouldn't we take them both?"

"That's not fair," Kohl said. "One for one, that's the rule."

"Life's not fair," T mumbled, but bent to help Vas heft the chair. Kohl picked up the cushions while Peebo left the typed note on the other chair.

Your *frumpy green armchair* has been repossessed... *To compensate, the universe has left you this very nice* ___TV___ . *Please enjoy!*

—The Uproots

T and Vas heaved the chair into the hallway—it was a good chair, really solid, really heavy, though not particularly good-looking. (T considered the sturdy-but-not-good-looking chair a kindred spirit and would be sad to see it go at the next exchange.) Peebo and Kohl slipped out the door and let it click shut behind them, but it caught and trapped T's sleeve.

"Damn it, my arm's stuck!" T hissed, letting Vas take all the weight of the chair. Kohl and T both tugged at the sleeve, but it was firmly shut in the door, which had locked itself behind them.

"Go on without me," T said.

"Don't be ridiculous!" Kohl took a pocketknife out of her jeans and sawed at T's sleeve until the arm was free and just a sliver of shirt hung from the doorframe.

"Oh my god, where's my Rolex?"

"Hilarious, T, good one," Kohl said.

The four of them carried the armchair and its cushions to Peebo's truck, right past the doorman, who actually *waved* and cheerfully wished them a good night. Vas and T managed to shove the chair into the bed of the truck, where Kohl covered it with a tarp to keep it nice. *Well, as nice as a pretentious, olive green, ugly-ass chair can be kept, anyway,* T thought. Peebo, Kohl and Vas got into the cab of the truck, and T rode in the open flatbed, holding onto the side and letting the stale night air buff every inch of exposed skin.

ONCE—IT SEEMED LIKE A VERY long time ago—T had had a different family, with a mother and father, two sisters and a brother, a squat little house on the edge of Philadelphia and a brown Plymouth Volare station wagon into which they all just barely fit.

T went to high school during the day and worked in the afternoons and evenings as a busser at the family's restaurant. Sometimes, on nights when it was slow, T, Monique and Seema, each with a stack of books, a notebook and a pencil, would do homework at a corner table. It became such a habit that it got hard to concentrate without the sisters' sniffling or the constant whine of canned music over the intercom. T got in trouble more than once for humming during a test.

As was expected, T had graduated from high school a semester earlier than everyone else. There'd been no ceremony, no excitement, not even a graduation celebration in T's family since they'd expected nothing less. When the diploma came in the mail, T's mother stuck it to the fridge with a magnet, as she'd done when Seema was five and had done some especially lovely crayon drawing. There hadn't even been tearful goodbyes with friends, since T was staying around for the extra semester, working full time in the restaurant, as if absolutely nothing had changed except T's schedule. If anyone wanted to see T again, all they had to do was order some pelau or stewed chicken. Nobody ever did.

There hadn't been money for college and, although T didn't get paid, sometimes the waitresses gave T a little cut of their tips for bussing. It wasn't much, but it was more than nothing. T had socked away every dollar in hopes of somehow making college a possibility.

Everyone but T had known where they were going in the fall. Colleges had made their decisions and the rich kids had already started packing up, buying new suitcases and new clothes to go in them, trying out new personalities and new hairstyles, studying bus maps of the wonderfully unfamiliar cities they'd soon call home. T had had no plan, no admissions offers, hadn't even made any applications because there hadn't been enough money to pay the ridiculous application fees. T had nothing except, as everyone was fond of saying, limitless potential.

When summer was halfway over, T's mother had cupped her hand around one of the balls of cinched hair on T's head, looked at T sadly, and said they should fix it.

"I like my hair the way it is," T had said.

"We need to fix this, doux doux, because nobody will give you a job like this. You'll be stuck with us at the restaurant forever," Wendy Persaud said. She fluffed the hair and let it bounce, smiling despite herself. "You're dougla, it's already a strike on you. Don't give them more. They will think you're foolish this way."

T squirmed away from Wendy, but not before she'd flattened the puff and said, "Maybe we can just braid it in rows. At least it will behave and look neat."

"No, Mooma, I'm keeping my hair the way it is," T said.

Wendy sighed, and ran her hand over her forehead. Her own hair was straight and shiny, pulled back tightly into a neat bun at the nape of her neck. "I have always let you do what you want, with the hair, with the clothes, but it's time to put that aside and think about other things now. You're grown. You need to find a job and take responsibility. Everything cannot be fashion, fashion, fashion anymore."

"It's not fashion," T said weakly. "It's important to me."

"You're being rebellious. You're making the wrong point."

"Mooma, I'm not trying to make a point. I'm trying to just *be*. You wouldn't understand; your hair's different."

Wendy ran the palm of her hand over her hair. "Eh, I got Mooma Ria's good hair," she said. "You got hair like your Bap." She crooked her mouth in sympathy and smoothed T's hair again, letting it spring back up when she took her hand away. "It's okay, doux doux. But it's time to act like a grownup and fix it. No more of this messing around, no more of this half-half buller business with boys and girls and any old cow. It's not fit. I love you, doux doux, but you have to decide to become someone true now. You can't have all the ways, all the choices all the time."

The next day, T had come home from the restaurant to discover that Wendy had thrown away most everything T owned—the hair elastics were gone, as were most of T's tops and scarves. Only two pairs of jeans and a couple T-shirts remained: a simple uniform fit for bussing tables. T's mother simply shrugged and pressed her lips together before saying, "Eh, eh. I told you. No more of this childish play."

T's father was locked in a tight game of All Fours with their neighbor Winston and his sons. They hunched over the kitchen table, a pot of tea and a plate of doubles between them, and barely looked up when T came stomping through the kitchen.

"Eh, eh, slow it down, you're going to put your feet right through the floor, stomping so hard!" Winston had said good-naturedly. His sons each grunted in T's direction, but didn't say anything, didn't pat T on the back or smile with recognition. T's father didn't look up from his cards.

"You gonna grow up now, owah?" T's mother called from the other room.

The next morning, T had packed the few remaining pieces of clothing into a bag, bought a Greyhound ticket to Pittsburgh, and left that family far behind.

WHEN THE DISPOSSESSED PRACTICED, IT was a holy mess, since there wasn't electricity for amps, even if they'd had them, and Kohl's guitar was missing the B string she couldn't afford to replace, and Peebo was still learning drums, and Vas was prone to conniptions when things weren't working right and was for the most part a pretty bad singer anyway. You couldn't even hear T's bass without the amps, so it felt pretty sad to keep *bong-bonging* on it underneath everything and that made T lose the rhythm too easily, and then the band would speed up and up and up like a runaway train because when they were in tune it felt effortless and the momentum was powerful. The sound felt so huge. They were making something together that was bigger than any of them could ever make alone. Even if it was awful, even if it was only tuneless recklessness and screaming, it was still powerful. It felt like freedom, and they all lost themselves to it too easily.

"You need self-control if you're going to have power," Kohl used to say. Nobody knew if she was quoting some big academic guy or if she'd invented that bit of wisdom for herself, but it made some sense.

In any case, not one of them had self-control, at least when it came to playing together.

It was hard to tell what the band was going to sound like when it finally performed, since this way The Dispossessed sounded less like the raging punks all of them wanted to be and more like a crappy recording of babies banging on pots and screaming into a tin can broadcast from somewhere in outer space.

They mostly did covers, Buzzcocks and Ramones and Blondie and Sex Pistols, but everybody was working on writing stuff too; it was just that nobody had finished anything enough to be tried out by the whole band. T had suggested the band just stick to covers anyway and call itself The Repeats, but Peebo had rejected that outright as Total Sell-Out Poseur Crap.

"T, man, you're messing us all up again."

"Don't call T 'man,' you jerk. T's asked you, like, a million times," Kohl said, kicking Peebo's leg with the blunt toe of her sloppy gold ballerina flat.

"I can't hear myself play without an amp," T said, ignoring the whole exchange. It got tiring to keep correcting and correcting people about the *him or her* issue, and it got kind of humiliating to keep trying when someone seemed deliberately obtuse about it. *Resistance is futile,* T thought. *We have ways of making you—*

"This used to be fun," Kohl said. "When did it get so ridiculous?"

"Serious isn't ridiculous," Peebo said under his breath.

"Practicing makes no sense this way," Vas said. "Waste of time." He threw his drumsticks on the floor, stormed to the fridge, and reached for the pack of cigarettes the band kept on top of it. (The fridge, with no electricity to run it, had become a giant plastic cupboard. used its shelves to store his neatly folded clothes. The rest of them refused to do the same, since everything came out of there smelling of plastic and mildew.)

"Outside!" Peebo yelled.

"Right. Your precious voice," Vas grumbled, stuffing himself into the hot pink puffer jacket he'd stolen off a store display. It was about two sizes too small and a revolting color with a now-dingy white stripe down each sleeve, but this only seemed to make Vas prouder, as if he wanted it to be obvious he'd stolen the jacket. Just like those poor people who steal cat food to eat instead of just stealing people food: kind of transparently all for show.

"I have work to do," Kohl said. "This is wasting my time. It's Professor Nat Hino's class tomorrow."

"All hail the Great *Professorina* Hino," Vas said, bowing.

"Don't be a pig," T said.

"*Professor* Nat Hino *is* great, you ass," Kohl said, undoing her guitar strap. "Greater than you could hope to be."

Vas snorted. "We *know* her name, you can just call her Professor Hino. You don't need to add her first name every time like she's some queen of something."

Kohl glared at Vas while she silently wound the guitar strap into a coil and stuffed it into the guitar bag. "I'm done," she said again. "I have too much work to do to pay attention to this."

"We're either going to have to rob a music store or sell some blood to get amps," T said, as if the conversation hadn't just gone sour.

"Then steal a generator, too, because there's no electric for it anyway," Vas said. He tapped the cigarette packet against his palm, then shook out one cigarette and put the pack back on top of the fridge. "There's only two left. We need more tomorrow," he said and left.

"Maybe you could get them next time, since you smoke most of them!" Kohl yelled at the closed door. At the same time, T yelled,

"Yessir, Mr. Vasilakis, sir! More cigarettes for his lordship!" and saluted in the most sarcastic way possible.

"You joke, but I think he'd be fine with that title," Peebo said. It was a paltry attempt at making up.

"You're one to talk," Kohl said.

Peebo shrugged.

AT NIGHT, AS OFTEN AS not, Kohl curled up in T's improvised blanket tent and peeled off her top, and the two of them slept skin-to-skin. Sometimes it was completely peaceful and simple; sometimes Kohl cried softly into T's shoulder while T pretended to sleep; sometimes Kohl and T tried desperately to whisper through the grunts and rude, smacking sounds of Peebo and Vas doing whatever it was they occasionally did behind Vas's curtains. It was a strange family, but one T would never leave. There was a lot of pushing and pulling, closer and farther apart, but still, when it came down to it, together was better and safer than alone. They clung together like a ball of fire ants.

Kohl was one of the few people who could touch T, and neither of them thought about it at all. Usually, it was hard: Somebody's hand or arm on T's body only made T more aware of the body and its ill fit, and it made T panicky, thinking about *where* the hand was, *what* it might touch, what lies that might tell someone about T. It was as though T's body was its own thing with its own agenda, or as if everybody just took it for granted that T's body was theirs to know. Kohl needed so much—to touch, to cry, to sleep, to be touched but not to be *used* for it—that she didn't pay much attention to T's body at all.

All of it—listening to Peebo and Vas getting it on, trying to pretend not to hear Kohl crying, even the sweetly calm nights of just holding her—made T feel lonely. It would be better to be completely alone, T thought, because at least then you could concentrate on yourself and your own thoughts, and not on the fact that there were people nearby but nobody close.

T WORKED SIX DAYS A week at a laundromat, which was one of the worst jobs T had ever had—long, boring days listening to the yammering of kids' programming and soap operas on the laundromat TV, the endless drone of the machines, the acrid flowers-and-bleach smell of detergent that never quite left T's nose. All of the chairs were like unyielding plastic ice cream scoops, except for the one busted office chair in the back, which at least had a little padding on the seat, even though the backrest was broken and you had to lean it against the wall to keep it from falling off when you sat down.

For a place where you went to clean things, it was really dirty; everything was caked in a layer of soap and grime that mixed together and made a thick, brown putty in the corners. Sometimes T saw roaches scuttling along the baseboards. The only stuff to eat, unless you brought your own food, was candy bars and syrupy orange juice from the vending machine. T didn't even get to do free laundry. When T wasn't staring into space and wishing for the day to end or trying to clean the lint out of one of the dryers without getting burned or shocked, T was making change for, or selling overpriced little packets of laundry detergent to, the irritated, haggard customers.

On the whole, the job sucked, except that T was left with long stretches of empty time in which all T had to do was sit there so everybody knew someone was watching the place. In those hours, T could read or write music or do a crossword or just stare into space and get hypnotized by the constant *whir-chunk-whir* of the washers.

Sometimes, if T was lucky, Kohl would stop in on a break from classes, bringing a doughnut and a couple cups of watery coffee, and the two of them would sit in the orange ice-cream-scoop chairs and watch the afternoon soaps while Kohl idly jotted notes on scrap paper like: *deconstruct soaps—gender* or *laundromat and claiming space* or simply *Chakravorty!* They had a few favorite laundry folks—the Furious Mom, who always brought one or more screaming children with her and was always, always yelling and covered in food splatter;

the Disaffected Youth, who took unreasonable care with ratty jeans that were probably incredibly expensive and simply designed to *look* secondhand; and the Proper Old Lady, who came in twice a week to wash one or two dainty pieces of clothing and sat in the corner of the laundromat ignoring the TV but watching everyone else with wide, interested eyes.

Despite all this, more often than not, T went home more tired than when T went in, feeling grimy, ears still humming from the constant low-level noise, and all for cruddy pay and the general humiliation of having to wear a logo-emblazoned red polo shirt and matching visor.

"Why don't you just quit?" Kohl had asked once as the two took turns licking the sugar off a glazed doughnut. It was gross, but still pretty good.

"Can't. If I quit, how are you gonna pay tuition next semester? How are we gonna afford food and stuff?"

"I can work too, you know," Kohl had said. She twisted her earring, something she only did when she was really worrying. "I'm not totally useless, and it might be good for you to have a break."

"You can't work *and* go to school. It would be a waste of school," T scoffed. "Plus, if I stop, I'll never be able to start again. Inertia." The laundromat was a veritable study in inertia, filled with dregs, the stuck and hopeless, the forgotten and the wasted. Nothing moved there except the clothes in the machines, and they only spun around and around.

"If you stopped working here, you could probably write more, compose stuff, and maybe the band would get good enough that you could just do that full time."

"The band isn't getting *that* good," T said with an eye roll. "It's just for fun." T passed Kohl the slobbery doughnut.

"Is it? Fun?" Kohl asked. T's eyes rolled as if they had a mind of their own.

"Maybe you could hock stuff from the Uproots work."

T gave her a stern look. "We *don't* steal. We just shift stuff around. We're not criminals; we're agitators." Outside the office window, washer lids and dryer doors slammed, the TV babbled, everything hummed.

"Yeah, but maybe we could get paid for our work once in a while. It's a lot of risk, and a lot of hauling stuff around." Kohl handed the doughnut back. "I'm done, by the way. You can finish it."

"We shouldn't get paid for doing something that's just the right thing to do. We're trying to make things better, not better ourselves."

"It costs us gas, you know, and time. And risk," Kohl said. "We're not indentured servants to the greater good."

"We're not criminals," T repeated lamely around the rest of the doughnut, barely a mouthful. "It doesn't mean much if it's no sacrifice." T choked on the doughnut a little—*a good lesson in not talking with one's mouth full,* T heard Wendy Persaud say—and Kohl held out a napkin. T took it and coughed into it for good measure.

"That's just about the stupidest thing I've ever heard. Of *course* it means something." Kohl sighed and pressed her lips to the back of T's neck. "The band's gonna make bank soon," she said. "You'll see. First thing, we'll pay for some real meds, instead of that back-alley crap you get."

"First thing, we're paying off your tuition. You never know when you'll need an actual trained English major for something," T said. "Plus, it's real Premarin. I just get it way cheaper from Dr. Not-a-Doctor."

"Those cheap hormones are probably from a horse or a dog or something," Kohl said.

"They're synthetic, like Twinkies. We love Twinkies."

Kohl didn't even crack a smile at that. "Premarin is dangerous. I've done the reading. You know it causes strokes? Death?"

"You know what else causes death? Suicide. Almost always. Plus, also cigarettes," T said. "But I don't see any of us stopping with the smoking."

"I would if I could," Kohl said. "Premarin isn't like nicotine, though. You're not addicted. You don't really need it."

T didn't even bother to say anything, but fixed Kohl with a glare that shouted *really?*

Kohl sighed. "Right. Still, I don't understand why you just don't go to the clinic and get them for free."

It was both a wise and unwise thing to say. The clinic *was* free, and T could get hormones there, prescribed and official—something safer than Premarin, too. But T just couldn't go in, register, and tell them, "No address, no last name." They might not give T any meds, or, worse, they might send the cops after them all for squatting.

"They're on your side. They're going to help you."

"What if they're not? Do you want me, really, to take that chance and get us all in trouble?" T asked.

"Those hormones from that guy on the street are going to kill you one of these days, and I'll sue your evil Dr. Feelgood if you die, you know." Kohl folded her arms across her chest and tried to look furious, but her eyes were shiny and a little wet, as though she might cry. T was irritated—it would make more sense to feel tenderness toward Kohl, but T couldn't muster that. It just seemed like another demand to make someone else feel better about T's decisions.

"We all gotta go sometime. If not hormones, then Twinkies. Better sooner and quicker and happily than later and slower and miserably." T shrugged. "Plus, then you can sue Dr. Not-a-Doctor and finally pay for some electricity or heat and maybe even that fancy college."

"I guess if you die young, you'll leave a beautiful corpse," Kohl said, her hand on T's chin. She tried to move closer to pet the back of T's head, but her sleeve stuck to the grimy counter. "It would just be good if it wasn't a choice between being alive and feeling okay."

"Yeah, but it don't mean a thing if it don't cost something. I'll be fine," T said, and rapped a fist on Kohl's head. "Knock wood."

CHAPTER 2

THE SHIFT

Dear homeowner:

Congratulations! Your possession has been Uprooted.

Do not be alarmed: you have not been robbed, nothing has been damaged and no one has been harmed; your __exercise bike__ has simply been repossessed by the universe... To compensate for the loss you probably feel, the universe has left you this very nice __armchair__ . Please enjoy!

—The Uproots

"That really wasn't an even exchange." Peebo smirked. "That was kind of dickish on our part."

T thought it was beside the point because the deed had long been done. They were spread out in various stages of recline across the squat, snickering idly about the job. The exercise bike lay in the bed of the truck parked on the street where anybody could take it. T, for one, didn't really care if someone *did* take it. It would be an interesting experiment, to see if anybody wanted it enough to haul the thing away.

"He was a douchebag for having an exercise bike in the first place," Vas said.

"Maybe he was recovering from a heart attack or something," Kohl said. "You don't know. You don't even know it was a 'he.'"

"Did you see the pictures on the mantle? That was a guy and that guy's a yuppie athlete. He's got a hundred-dollar helmet and a bright-orange fake tan and a receding hairline and a gross 1970s cop moustache. Guy's a turd."

"We're supposed to be an impartial force of the Universe," Kohl said, looking up from the papers she'd fanned out on the floor in front of her. "The Universe doesn't judge."

"The guy obviously goes to a tanning booth," Vas said. "The Universe *totally* judges." Vas stood behind the counter in the kitchen area drinking water directly from the plastic jug. He continued to do this despite very unsubtle dirty looks from both Kohl and T.

"Then why do people like that always seem to win?" T said. "The rest of us get cancer or get hit by trucks, and those folks just skate on by, drinking their wine coolers and wearing their paisley ties and laughing at beer commercials and slapping each other on the back. And *quit* that, it's disgusting!" T hurled a wadded-up T-shirt at Vas. Vas smiled and kept drinking.

"But *we* have the true gift of *friendship!*" Kohl said, as if reciting something. "Who's rich and who's poor *now*?"

"Nope, that guy is still totally rich," T said.

Peebo shrugged and went back to tearing the newspaper into little strips and piling them on the floor.

"What the hell are you doing, anyway?" Kohl asked.

"Pillow," Peebo said. He held up his pillow in one hand and a fistful of the newsprint in the other, then crumpled the paper and jammed it into the pillowcase. "It's getting flat. My neck is killing me."

"That's a fire hazard," T said.

"So are you," Vas said, capping the water jug and belching loudly in T's direction.

"Is that supposed to be a *flamer* joke?" Kohl was on her feet in seconds. "Totally violent! Plus, pot, kettle, black, dude!" She shoved him with her foot.

"Not gay," said Vas.

"Could've fooled me, man," Peebo snorted.

Vas stomped to the door and crammed his feet into his shoes. "Pay phone. Back soon," he mumbled before ducking out.

Peebo glared at the banged-up door as it shuddered closed, then went back to stuffing his pillow.

Nobody seemed to hear it when T said, "*I'm* not gay, you know."

A few minutes passed in which Peebo and Kohl bent to their tasks. T watched Peebo, eyes narrowed. The only sounds were the scratch of Kohl's pencil and the tear of paper as Peebo pulled the newspaper into strips.

Then Kohl smacked her pencil down and looked up. "What if we got a camping stove?" she asked. "You know, like a butane thing?"

"With what money?" Peebo said.

"I'm sure we could pool something together."

"Those little butane canisters are spendy," T said.

"I'm just trying to make things a little better," Kohl said. "We could use it to cook and also to get warm when it's freezing." She picked up the pencil and scribbled a bit, barely glancing at what she was writing. She looked like a robot—a scrawny, angry robot with half a head of hair. A robot built to scowl and study English, for some reason.

"I like body heat," T said, just before the door banged open. Vas, his arms raised in victory, ran at Kohl, aiming to kiss her. She jerked sideways, and Vas's mouth landed somewhere in the snarls of hair at her cheek.

"I got it!" Vas shouted, bouncing across the room like an untethered pony, sending plastic crates skidding in his wake.

Kohl went to the front door and closed it. "You can't leave the door hanging open like that," she said. "Meanwhile, got *what*, you unabating nutjob?"

"That's *Manager* Nutjob to all you *hoi polloi* now," Vas said gleefully, then went dancing off to the bathroom. They heard the shower screech to life.

"He's going to be insufferable now," T said.

"Three minutes!" Kohl shouted toward the bathroom door. "Else there won't be enough for everyone!"

"How much longer you think the water's going to keep going?" Peebo said. "Eventually, the owner's going to figure out it's still on and stop paying, you know. We already lost electric."

"Until the water's off, I'm getting as washed as I can," Kohl said. "After that, baby wipes and spit. I figure I've got maybe two or three weeks of real showers left." She pulled a couple books from the pile on which she rested her chin, flipped pages as if she were looking for something important, then gave up and left them all fanned out in front of her. She threw her pencil down again—it seemed to be a dramatic gesture she'd perfected.

"Done with the books for the day?" T asked.

Kohl leaned over and shouted in the direction of the bathroom, "Two or three weeks of showers, unless somebody ruins it sooner!"

WHEN THEY FIRST MOVED INTO the squat, it was Vas who'd found the space, and Vas who'd busted the plate glass window so they could crawl in, and Vas who'd stolen the milk crates for furniture. The whole thing, even the band, had been Vas's idea.

The idea of the group's life had spread amongst them like an infection, and Vas was like patient zero. He found Peebo and pulled him in; Peebo convinced T to join them, and T brought Kohl. That was how it was supposed to work. Good ideas were supposed to be catching like that. They had felt wild and strong, unstoppable. It was thrilling to become something larger together, to do something important. *Dangerously* important.

The afternoon it had all started, when Vas met Peebo, was mostly like every afternoon Vas had to endure working at the office supply store. It *was*, at least, until four o'clock, when Vas sneaked out into the alley for a smoke and found Peebo tucked in with the trash there.

Peebo had been sleeping off the day, waiting out the heat in the safest place he could find as far away from his family's place as possible. He didn't want anybody he knew to see him like this: dirty, sleepy, heaped in with the trash like a junkie.

His family had held much higher hopes for him. They'd given up most of what they owned in Taiwan just to take him to the States... to Pittsburgh, of all places, *seriously*, but there was some cousin or uncle or someone already living in Pittsburgh who was going to help them with whom they never actually wound up connecting. Now they all lived together in a couple rooms above the small grocery where his mother worked: his parents, him, his older brother De-Wei, a couch on which their mother slept, a few mats on the floor for the rest of them, a pot to cook in. In Taiwan, they'd had a maid and soft, high beds and wheat-colored carpet. There had been a sister there, too, Jiao, but she was too young and was left in Taiwan in the care of an aunt.

When he decided to leave the family, he left for good, because he knew his mother wouldn't let him go, and his father wouldn't take him back. He hated the fancy private college that cost more in a year than any of them ever dreamed of having in the United States, the one where he had miserably been studying computer programming because his parents knew that it was a good, sturdy profession he could learn to do well and that he would earn enough to support the whole family when he did.

He'd faced a lifetime doing a thing he hated just because he loved his mother. And then he failed two semesters in a row and was asked to leave the department, which meant he could stay in school but had to switch majors, and all that tuition money was going to be sunk instead into some overpriced business degree that would be more useless to him than it was expensive. So he ripped up the letter from school, flushed it, and dropped out officially. His parents probably wouldn't have read it anyway since reading in English was sometimes slow going, but he thought it better to get rid of it entirely so there was no evidence of him at all and he would be easier to erase from family history. He packed a few T-shirts and pairs of underwear into a plastic grocery bag, then took the refunded tuition and hid it in an envelope in a kitchen cupboard where only his mother was sure to find it. De-Wei was pretty short and couldn't reach that high, and his dad never went in there at all.

"DUDE, YOU OKAY?" VAS HAD kicked the guy's foot to see if he was alive. It was the only thing sticking out from behind the heaps of empty boxes and the bent and rusting stacks of old shelving.

"Sorry," the guy said, and scrambled up, ready to go.

"No, man, it's fine. You should stay if you want. I won't tell anybody." Vas offered him a cigarette as a symbol of friendliness, but the guy shook his head. There was a streak of something awful and reddish-brown on his neck. He was, Vas thought, so dirty.

"I'm on my way; just give me a minute."

"Suit yourself," Vas said. "You eat yet?"

The guy shot him a look to mark just exactly how ridiculous that question was, so Vas said, "Hang out here for just a minute," then left and returned with a plastic container of orange-colored casserole. It said DONA in shaky marker strokes on the lid. "Stole it from the employee fridge. It's been in there since yesterday."

The guy looked grateful, took the lid off, and scooped out some of the casserole with two fingers. Vas waggled the fork at him, but he didn't even seem to notice it. "Thanks, man, this is amazing. Who's Dona?"

"I have no idea. No Dona works with *me*. Maybe in photocopying?" Vas tried to lean casually against the dumpster, but the smell made him gag, so he crossed his arms over his chest, cocked his chin, and leaned against the brick wall next to the door. A sign above his head read: LOADING ZONE NO PARKING. He popped the collar of his red work polo and hoped it looked nonchalant.

"She spells her name wrong. Poor Dona. Probably why she's working there and not at a better job."

Vas laughed, and then the guy looked horrified and said, "Oh, man, I'm sorry! I didn't mean it like that."

"It's fine," Vas said, and it seemed as if it really was. "Everyone who works there is an idiot."

The guy barely stopped shoveling food into his mouth to look up. Vas thought that underneath all that dirt he was probably okay-looking in a stretched-out, too-tall kind of way. He stunk, though, like sourness and decay. The alley probably wasn't helping. The dumpster vomited its trash onto the pavement; unbagged garbage was everywhere, rotting in heaps.

"Except you, right?" the guy said, starting to shovel food into his mouth again. "Everyone *but you* is an idiot."

"Jury's still out."

The guy snorted and turned back to the food. He ate the whole container of Dona's lunch in minutes, using only his fingers. He looked at Vas when it was empty and gave a paltry half-smile while dropping his eyes to Vas's hips.

Vas held up his hands, "No, man, no nothing needed for me. Just figured you were hungry."

At that, the homeless guy looked relieved. Vas invited him to crash at his place. After a little convincing, it was agreed that the guy would wait for him in the alley until Vas was through with work.

When Vas was finally free of irritating business, he went back to the alley, half expecting to find it empty. But the gangly guy was still there, huddled in with the trash. He was pawing through the cardboard as if he'd lost something. Vas figured he was just doing it to do something, because he looked as though he didn't have anything to lose in the first place.

"I'm Vas," he said, in order to announce his presence, patting the kid's back and startling him.

"Pi-ao," the homeless guy said.

Vas looked at him oddly, one eyebrow raised.

"Pi-ao," he said again, slow and loud, as if he were talking to a child. "My name is Pi-ao."

Vas laughed. "I thought you were saying *meow* at me, like a cat or something."

The guy furrowed his brows and looked irritated. "Okay, man, thanks for the food and stuff. I gotta go. There's a good place in the Giant Eagle parking lot, and I don't want somebody else to get it."

"Hey, no offense, I'm sorry. You just surprised me, and I thought you were crazy, or I was going crazy, or something. What was it... Pee-bo? Like Peabo Bryson?" Vas said.

Pi-ao looked at Vas for a long, uncomfortable moment, as if he were making some kind of calculated measure of his soul, then sighed and shrugged. He looked so defeated, Vas thought.

"Yeah," he said. "Peebo's fine."

AFTER A WEEK, VAS AND Peebo had discovered T at the laundromat. While their clothes whirled clean in a machine, Vas and Peebo talked idly with T, who figured the conversation would at least be more amusing than watching the machines and making change. Vas gave them a crash course in beginner Marxism and political resistance and the most effective kinds of activism and other stuff he had spent his time thinking about before dropping out of Pitt. T could have listened to that nice, white, rich kid talk about the trouble with private property all day long, and never once thought about the fact that Vas' shoes probably cost more money than T saw in a month. Since leaving home, T had been cobbling together the weeks, sleeping on a couch here, a spare cot there, a linoleum floor in the intervals between lucky breaks. Sometimes it was easier to sleep at the laundromat desk during the day, bumping awake when a customer knocked on the counter and drowsing back to sleep just as quickly when the exchange was complete, and then stay up all night to wander and scrounge. Time had a strange, slipping quality that way, as if the moments that made up a day had been slapped together carelessly and without order.

By the time their clothes were dry, Vas had decided that the three of them should form an activist band, even though nobody played any instruments. Peebo and T were both on board.

Quite quickly during the laying of plans, they realized they had no instruments, no songs, and no talent of which to speak. Vas volunteered to write the music and sing but thought they needed one more person, because every rock band had two guitars, Vas was not about to sing *and* play guitar, and Peebo had already called drums; so that left T and one other person they'd need. All T knew music-wise was how to play the recorder from sixth grade music class, which meant T had a repertoire of three songs, with "Three Blind Mice" topping the list. They needed someone else.

T thought of the girl from the laundromat.

When T found her again—well, really, when Kohl found T, because she came into the laundromat brandishing some awful-looking iced and sprinkled neon-colored doughnut and offering T half even though they'd only met the one time before when T had sold her a packet of powdered detergent for the washers—T pulled her behind the counter and proceeded to make a case for the band.

"I'm in," she said, even though T hadn't done much more than mention a band in which none of the members was properly qualified to participate.

"I even play guitar already," she said. "I taught myself. I can teach you, too, if you want. It's easy. They let you play the display guitars at Guitar Czar."

It was a pretty good idea. All they had to do after that was get their hands on some instruments, learn to play them, write some songs, find a place to practice, get really good, and have themselves booked for some decent gigs.

"IF YOU GET ME TO eat that doughnut, I'll give you a hundred dollars!" the girl in the cage shouted.

T stopped to look. The girl was sallow-skinned and bony, folded into a large dog cage with a thermos of water and a towel and nothing else. Her stringy yellow hair was inexpertly streaked with pink, so that she looked like a strangely colored, mousy little tiger swimming in a polyester slip dress. She'd probably gotten the dress at a Goodwill, since it looked to be older than she was.

"You win a hundred dollars if you can get me to eat that doughnut," she said more quietly.

T looked at the doughnut, which had been bought at a crappy doughnut chain a couple blocks from the library. It was definitely nothing special, not even a flavor T liked much, since the blueberry bits inside were freeze-dried and felt like nuggets of sand, but it had been in the going stale "half-price" bin at the shop, and T had planned to spend the hour before the shift at the laundromat sitting on a bench under a tree by the library with the blue-gray doughnut. It had cost almost twenty minutes' earnings, but T had found a five-dollar bill crumpled up on the ground under a car tire on the way there and decided to splurge. T laid the doughnut in its napkin carefully beside the girl's cage.

"You can just have it," T said. "I don't need the money. You should just eat it."

"Twenty-eight percent of the world lives in poverty and couldn't afford that doughnut!" she shouted as T started to walk away. "Poor people can't buy fancy doughnuts!"

"You don't have to buy it. I'm giving it to you."

"I'm not poor, I'm making a point."

T sighed, turned around, and dropped to sit on the grass next to the girl's open cage.

"What's the point you're making?"

"People are starving." The girl had wrapped her bony fingers around the bars of the cage and pressed her face against them. She reminded T of Gretel, locked in the witch's cage, doomed—except this girl was so skinny, with stringy hair and strangely small teeth.

"Instead of giving away a hundred dollars to someone for making you eat," T said, "you could just donate the money to a soup kitchen and feed a bunch of people."

"Nobody ever wins. Nobody makes me eat. I don't even have the money," she admitted. "It just makes people pay attention, makes 'em think about the issue, and maybe they'll do something, and tell their friends to do something…" The girl quirked her mouth, as if to say "*Et cetera, et cetera.*"

"You don't eat?" T asked, shifting on the grass to get a little more shade. The tree overhead rattled its already-browning leaves.

"No," the girl said. "Just juice and broth, mostly. I'm a hunger artist."

"Like in Kafka?" T asked.

The girl's eyes widened. "You know it?"

"That guy dies in the end, and nobody's paying attention to him. And he says he doesn't eat because he doesn't like food. There's no point and no effect except his death," T said. "Tenth grade lit class."

The girl waved it off. "I've got a point. There's a point. I can't be ignored forever."

"You must be new here," T said wryly. The girl chuckled and shook her head.

Behind them, the river chopped at the concrete shore, sending up a sickening fish smell that probably wasn't fish. Algae seemed to cover everything near the water with its green slime. A couple boats dipped up and down in the distance, but otherwise the water looked empty, even of gulls. Two kids ran crazy circles around a woman who was probably their mother, for all she was screaming at them. *Maybe a nanny*, T thought, and sniffed. The river was a weird place, a mix of the grossly low and snobby rich.

"Don't you eat even in secret? A little, so you can keep going?" T asked after a minute of silence.

"Principles are principles, even if nobody's looking," the girl said with a superior tilt of her chin. She tapped the thermos of water.

29

"It probably wouldn't affect anything if you ate a little, at least when you're not here. Nobody would know."

"It would affect *me,* and *I* would know," the girl said earnestly. T noticed her knees, which were so bony they were almost pointed; the sharp edges of her kneecaps threatened to cut through the loose skin. She widened her eyes. "Take the doughnut back, please! You probably need it!"

"Nah, I'm fine," T said, climbing back up and dusting off. "Keep it for show. Or give it to somebody else. Good luck."

AT THE END OF THE day, T locked up the laundromat, took the envelope of saved-up cash, and went to the river where Nah hung out. Kohl called him Dr. Not-a-Doctor, but he made everyone he knew call him Nah. The runaway kids hung around him at the river like mall rats who'd lost their mall. He didn't mess with pot or coke or any of the normal drugs, but he could always be counted on for the more interesting stuff like black beauties or X and he kept T and a few of the other kids supplied with Premarin.

"Lala, looking sweet today," he said when T handed over the envelope. "You ever wanna come work for me, you got it. My girls get top money."

Nah made T's skin crawl. He was nearly as wide as he was tall, with a sparse pencil scribble of a moustache and hair slicked into a tight bun at the back of his tiny head. He wore, without fail, a too-large T-shirt draped over a ratty pair of shin-length, silky basketball shorts. The shirt was always the same one, with a sexy cartoon cat and an obscene phrase on it that was probably supposed to be funny. Cinched over the whole ensemble, Nah wore a fanny pack from which he pulled his merchandise and into which he deposited wads of cash.

He called absolutely everybody Lala. T figured he couldn't be bothered to remember names—or perhaps he was so fried from testing his own merchandise he no longer had the brain power to do it.

He looked ridiculous, but he was always clean. His teeth were white and straight, and his nails were always trimmed. He looked like somebody's rich-but-crappy, spoiled teenaged son. The drug-and-girl stuff was, T thought, most likely a side hustle his family knew nothing about. Nah would have been laughable, except that he wore a handgun in the waistband of his jeans and was fond of lifting his shirt to show it off.

So T smiled and nodded, gave the money, took the package—tried to make the whole thing go as fast as possible.

"Always so standoffish," Nah said, shaking his head and running a finger down T's arm. A line of hair stood on end where Nah had touched. One of the girls leaning against Nah's shoulder—T knew her only as Lala, like everyone else— clucked her tongue and swiped her dirty hair out of her face.

"Pity, pity," Nah said. "See you again real soon." T hurried away from Nah and went back up the river path. A few blocks up, the girl was still crouched in her cage, the doughnut untouched beside her.

"You again," she called. "Afro Puffs!"

The name sent a clench of irritation up T's spine, as if this wispy stranger had taken something that didn't belong to her. If it had been anyone but this caged and frail little girl, T might have… probably slunk away grumbling. It would be too exhausting, picking up the fight every time someone said something ignorant. T would have time for nothing else.

T swerved off the sidewalk and onto the grassy bank. "It's me," T said in a tight voice.

"Was your day a good day?"

"I work at a laundromat."

"Was your day a day, then?"

T nodded. "It was a day. I have them all the time. There are lots of days. How goes the artistry? Still successfully hungry?" T unlatched the door to the cage and opened it, then realized how ridiculous a gesture that was—it did nothing, as the girl stayed where she was, and T was not about to crawl into the cage with her. At least T could look her in the eye without wire bars in the way.

"Nobody—not a single person—has stopped all day except you. I've just been baking here in the sun like a Virginia ham."

"Quit for the night," T said, offering a hand. "You don't sleep out here, do you?"

"No," she sighed. "I take everything back to my place and sleep there." She must have been freezing—the sun had begun to drop low on the horizon, and the air had gotten chilly without it. T kept hearing Wendy Persaud's voice: *The girl has no meat on her bones to keep her warm. No sense under all that candy-blondie hair.* She had no sweater, either—nothing but the cage and the chipped blue thermos, which lay on its side near the girl's thigh.

"Where's your place?"

"The YW on Fifth." The girl's face was a bit ashamed and a bit proud. She quirked her sparse eyebrows and lifted her chin in a pointy little challenge, but her arms wrapped around her chest protectively. It was as if she was looking for a fight but afraid to find one.

"You're not staying in a shelter. I have a place."

"What do you want for it?" she asked warily. Her arms pulled tighter. "I don't *do* anything, if that's what you're after."

T looked at her as if she was crazy. "Are you kidding? I don't want anything. It's just safe, and nobody will bother you, unless you're really bothered by jerks, because two out of the three people I live with are jerks."

"I'm Twee," she said, holding out her hand through the open cage door.

"T."

"T what?"

"My name. It's T."

"Got it," Twee said and left it at that. T's jaw loosened. "But I'm gonna call you Puffs." She reached up and fluffed one of the elastic-bound balls of pink hair on T's head. "Afro Puffs if I'm feeling formal."

T pulled back. "T, seriously, please, just T."

When Twee raised her eyebrows, T said, "I'm not a pet."

Twee shrugged and let her hand drop as if it was no big deal, but her face fell. That was the end of it. Usually, T had to endure a long conversation to explain the name and—usually—about a million other things the other person wanted to know about, stuff that was, in general, none of anybody's business. But Twee simply nodded, crawled out of the cage, and started to fold it up. She had a luggage cart to which she strapped the flattened cage, and the whole apparatus, when broken down, didn't look terribly cumbersome or heavy. She wheeled it behind her as if it was nothing.

"Do you want me to take that for you?" T said. "You know, since you're not eating lately and probably super weak?"

Twee scoffed. "I've got it, thanks." As if to prove her point, she heaved the cage forward and walked a little faster. She was short and very thin but, as the cliché went, quite surprisingly strong. T's mother would have called her *a slip of a girl*, and T finally found a way to make some sense of the phrase: Twee looked as flimsy and light as a lady's slip, as if a strong gust would blow her off into the sky, the way the wind sometimes took Wendy's slips off the clothesline and sent them whipping and cartwheeling down the road. With her clothes flapping as she went, Twee looked a little like that. The crate rumbled and bumped along the sidewalk, jumping the cracks in rhythmic jolts.

They walked away from the river, past the gothic-and-glass landscape of Pittsburgh's downtown, and along the way Twee pointed out all the best places to set up a cage and the places where she was routinely chased out when she did. They made it to the burned-out building that was the squat and climbed in through the broken plate glass window on the first floor. T took Twee into the stairwell and up to the third floor (after one flight she finally conceded to help lugging the cage up the stairs) and kicked open the apartment door with a flourish.

"Home, crappy home!" T said grandly, with a sweeping, Price Is Right Showcase Model kind of gesture.

Twee looked around. "It's really nice. It's huge, and you guys fixed it up really good."

"It still smells like burned toast, but it works." T pushed the cage against the wall, kicked off both shoes, and went to join Kohl at the counter island, the one at which they usually sat to chat while cooking in the island's sink. It was a small kitchen space—just a counter, a few cupboards, and, in the corner, a non-working fridge, plus the stand-alone counter at which Kohl worked. The counters and cupboards were the same awful white, though the Formica countertops had been smattered with some sort of gold flake, which was probably intended to make it look like ritzy marble but ended up giving the effect of booth seats at a roller rink.

"Hey," said Kohl, gesturing with a spoon from where she stirred another horrible-looking concoction. She had a little fire going in the sink with some charcoal Peebo had stolen from someone's barbeque grill. "Is it Muffy or Buffy?"

"Twee," Twee said, as if the sting of Kohl's words hadn't reached her. T thought that maybe it hadn't. Twee seemed so wispy, not entirely present.

"Oh, *Twee*, my bad," Kohl said.

"Stop it," T said and punched Kohl's arm a little harder than intended. Kohl furrowed her brows and mouthed *ow*. "Play nice," T said. "Twee's here to stay a while."

Kohl cocked her hip and rolled her eyes. "Too few white folks here? You trying to find Vas a friend?"

"What's with you?" T said. Kohl looked sloppy, loose, a little furious. Her face slipped sideways.

"Sorry, kid, sorry," she mumbled. "Vas was being a dick this morning. And then I had a shit day." She glugged something from a plastic cup.

"And somebody found something to drink, I see."

"Just water." Kohl sloshed the cup in T's direction. "Helped get rid of the cruddy vodka taste from earlier."

"Right." T pushed the cup to the other end of the counter.

"That's seriously just water, you jerk!" Kohl said, pulling it back. "Don't try to oppress me. I've had enough of that in my life, *Mom*."

Twee raised her eyebrows, and T gestured to Kohl.

"Bengali parents," T said in answer.

"Asian contingent, loud and only a little proud but mostly just tired," Kohl said, saluting with the spoon.

"And you're part of the contingent, too, I assume," Twee said to T.

"You keeping track, Snow?" Kohl snorted.

"Ignore her. I'm half only," T said. "Which is like being an Easter Christian, or a mermaid." T sniffed the pot of whatever-it-was Kohl was stirring, then pulled back quickly, eyes watering from the sulfurous glop. Twee was too busy to notice the cartoonish move—she ran her hands along the edges of the counter and cupboards as if she'd never seen anything like them before—but Kohl scowled at T and clucked her tongue.

"Don't let T fool you," Kohl said. "T is in the club."

"I pay the dues, but they won't let me in the clubhouse without a member to escort me."

"You're Caribbean, right?" Twee said, tapping her ear. "I hear it in there. Trinidad? That's like Asian Lite." She hopped and pulled herself up to sit on the counter behind them. T tried to face them both, at least a little, but Kohl didn't move and kept her back to Twee.

"You really earned that Orientalist badge in Girl Scouts, didn't you!" Kohl snapped.

"Shut your mouth," T said to Kohl. Then, to Twee, "I'm island to the core: half East Indian, half West Indian, half white, maybe Irish or something."

"That's more than two halves," Twee pointed out.

"T is a rule-breaker," Kohl said.

"Traditional Bengalis?" Twee asked Kohl.

"Don't even know anymore. Used to be, anyway." Kohl wiped her hands on the front of her jeans and then picked up the spoon. "Left home and haven't seen them in seven years. Don't care to, either. Assholes. They wanted a boy."

T knocked Kohl hard on the shoulder. "Show some respect. It's still family."

"Could've fooled me," she said. "Besides, I don't need them. *This* is my real family. Now I've got two jerk brothers and you." She nuzzled T's nose with her own, then stabbed at the cooking fire a few times with the spoon, trying to get it to glow hotter. The stainless-steel pit of the sink was stained a powdery black from all the previous cooking efforts. T tried to keep looking serious, but inside every organ and muscle felt warm and glowing. It *was* a family—a contentious, holding-together, irritation of a family. Which was pretty much just "family" by most lights. As much as they bickered and clashed, T knew, they'd invited T into the home and made a space for T that fit just right. They teased mercilessly, but they'd never ask T to be any different.

"I don't blame you," Twee said softly, and Kohl's shoulders dropped a little.

T turned to Twee. "That's Kohl. Believe it or not, she's *not* one of the jerks I told you about. She's the one non-jerk here."

Kohl beamed. "Flatterer!" She tossed the spoon down, skipped over to throw her arms around T, and laid a wet kiss on T's neck. "I love this one! Always not calling me a jerk and sweet stuff like that!" T stiffened, and Kohl noticed, whispered "Sorry, doll," and dropped her arms.

"I can see why you'd be head over heels," Twee said, holding out a hand. "You seem like good people."

"High friends and low standards." Kohl smiled genially, turning back to the pot without shaking Twee's hand. Despite her mood, it seemed more like an oversight than an insult. "Almost done with food, if you guys want. It will probably be disgusting, but it also probably won't kill you."

"You're spectacular," T said, laying a threadbare blanket on the floor. "We only have one bowl each, so you and I can share, Twee, if you're not afraid of cooties."

"I love cooties," Twee said. She swept the floor a bit with her foot, then sat down cross-legged. "Especially chocolate chip cooties."

"I see what you did there," T said, and sat down next to her. "Good job."

"She's a nice one," Kohl relented. "She can play."

"Twee's going to stay the night." T scooted closer to Twee and nudged her gently with a foot. She smiled, and T smiled back at her and winked, as if they were both in on a secret. There was no earthly reason to do it—there was no secret—but it felt kind of nice, kind of safe, to try it with Twee.

"Then where am *I* supposed to sleep?" Kohl asked. She'd caught the wink, too, and was looking at T strangely, as if she was happy and sad all at once.

"In your own bed for a change." T threw a wadded-up piece of newspaper in her direction. It fell disappointingly short. Kohl snorted and turned back to the sink.

Twee pointed back and forth between them and raised her eyebrows. "Are you two…?"

"Not really," T said.

"Not really *at all*," Kohl said. "It's just convenient sometimes."

"Except for the convenient part," T said. "You're not convenient and you're not much help."

"Not my fault you're all no-touchy-touchy. Your choice to be stone."

"I'm not stone. I'm just picky, and I don't like you very much," T said.

Food was dished out—T noticed Kohl had spooned quite a bit more than a single fair share into T's bowl—and the three sat together on the blanket to eat.

When she saw that Twee wasn't touching the food, Kohl said, "I know it's not gourmet, but it's not horrible, either."

"Oh, no! No comment on the food at all!" Twee said. She pulled her knees up to her chest and wrapped her stringy arms around them. She dropped her chin to rest between her kneecaps, and it made her chin look sharper so her face looked just like a cartoon heart. "I just don't eat."

When Kohl looked perplexed, T said, "Hunger artist. Like in Kafka."

"It's a political protest," Twee said.

"Isn't there a way to protest *and* eat? Your protest is going to kill you. You're thin as a rail."

"I'm small-boned," Twee said, sounding a bit proud. "It just shows on me faster than other people."

Kohl looked unsure but nodded. "Okay. But you won't last long in this city if you don't eat. The winters are freezing, even inside, at least in this crappy hole." Kohl glared at the bare floor, the bare walls, the sparse, plastic crate furniture. "There might as well not be windows at all, as drafty as they are. And there are a lot of hills out there. You need energy."

Twee smiled. "I'll eat when I have to," she said.

T waved a forkful of glop at Twee. "You *have* to try this," T said. "My darling, please take this cabbage as a symbol of my undying love!"

"Oh! There's carrot, too! You must really be serious! I hear you don't give your carrot to just anyone." Twee clasped her hands under her chin and batted her eyes. Kohl rolled hers and let her head drop to the counter.

"No, my blossoming lotus flower. And if you look, you'll see that's real twenty-four-carrot, too!"

"All right, already, ha ha," Kohl said from the countertop; she didn't even lift her head, so it came out a bit muddled. "I'd dump dinner on your heads just for that pun, if I didn't mind wasting good food."

"'Good' is a matter of some debate," T said, and shoveled up a forkful of glop.

AFTER ALL THE PLATES HAD been wiped clean and put on the shelf, Twee perched on a window ledge to watch as Vas swept a small space clear with his foot, kicking the rubble of milk crates and stray shoes to the side. In the empty space, Peebo pulled out a single snare drum, one cymbal, and two plastic tubs and set them up together like a drum kit. Both Peebo and Vas were still lobbing brief and threatening glances in Twee's direction like leery cats, as ready to fight as to flee. Vas actually seemed to puff up a few sizes whenever Twee's eye fell on him, and he was extra bossy about where to put the equipment and who should be doing what. Kohl and T leaned together to tune their guitars to the same almost-in-tune note. In a few moments they were ready to go, and Vas took his place at the imaginary microphone, clasped his hands around nothing, and fixed Twee with his best steely-hot lead singer glare.

They played for their audience of one, who hollered and waved her arms and danced around as if trying to make up for being only one person. Vas rocked from foot to foot and crooned in some combination of Morrison and Morrisey. Everything felt easy, loud, and good. They made it all the way through their set from "Jellyfish Heart" to "Colombian Necktie" without anyone screwing up, and Twee yelled her heart out when they finally decided to pack everything up and quit for the night because Vas's throat had started to hurt.

THAT NIGHT, KOHL DROPPED A blanket over the edge of the counter, pinned the sides of it to the floor with a couple shoes, and slept in the makeshift tent. T felt the gesture like the gift it was probably meant to be. When Twee lay down next to T in the tent, T shoved the pillow and blanket toward her.

"Don't be ridiculous." Twee pushed the pillow back under T's head, wrapped herself around T, and laid her head against T's shoulder. She was wearing the same little dress she'd worn all day, and T figured it was probably horribly uncomfortable. Her leg lay low on T's thigh, her arm curled around T's belly, and T thought about how subtly she was avoiding the zones of T's body where a hand might be too much. T dropped a kiss onto Twee's cheek in thanks. She traced a line along T's jaw; her finger slid gently against the skin.

"Soft," she whispered.

"Mmmm," T said.

"You ever get hair there?"

"No," said T, stiffening. It always started this way, with questions that seemed innocent even as they were meant to pry and which quickly escalated into more and more invasions.

"*I* do, sometimes, like heavy peach fuzz," she said. Her finger continued to draw back and forth along the bone of T's jaw. "The girls at school used to call me Grizzly Adams and say I had a beard. But it's just that my hair's naturally a lot. It used to make me cry, though."

T started to loosen again. Twee wasn't on a mission; Kohl was nearby; the blanket made a soft cocoon around them, turning the room outside dim pink-orange; and T was safe and sleepy. Twee's finger slowed. She brought her knee to rest against T's hip and her breathing deepened. After a while, she stopped moving and her weight against T's shoulder was a firm pressure that held everything, for the moment, perfectly still.

CHAPTER 3

THE EFFING TACO

Dear homeowner:

Congratulations! Your possession has been Uprooted.

Do not be alarmed: you have not been robbed, nothing has been damaged and no one has been harmed; your <u>shiny stainless-steel blender</u> has simply been repossessed by the universe... To compensate for the loss you probably feel, the universe has left you this very nice <u>exercise bike</u> . Please enjoy!

—The Uproots

PS: The exercise bike is way better for you—protein shakes never helped anybody's health!

TWEE HAD ADDED THAT LAST part to the note after Peebo left it on the kitchen counter. She'd talked her way into coming along, despite Peebo's strenuous objections, and she was supposed to be just observing and helping lift stuff.

"Great advice from someone on a hunger strike," Vas mumbled.

"I *told* you guys this would be a problem," Kohl hissed at T's back. They had all crowded at the end of the hallway to wait for the elevator down, which was a risk they didn't often take. But it was the seventh floor and clomping down that much stairwell would probably draw more attention. Kohl spat viciously into the ashtray near the elevator.

"As if I could have stopped her!" T hissed back.

"Whatever, you guys," Twee said. "If Peebo had done it, you would think it was fine, Vas."

"Peebo wouldn't have done it," Vas said, giving Peebo a significant look.

Peebo shifted the blender on his hip. "Jeez, hurry up," he mumbled, pressing the elevator button a few more times. Nothing happened.

"Let's just take the stairs," Kohl said. She held the heavy fire door open with her back, letting everyone else pass her into the echoing stairwell. Shiny gray paint was glopped all over the stairs, the handrails, the walls. "Wait. Holy crap!"

"What?" T whispered.

Kohl turned to Twee. "Did you close the door when we left the apartment?"

"I don't know," Twee said, already poised between the first and second stair. "Does it matter? Someone's going to figure out we were there."

"Yeah, but hopefully not before we get far away," Vas said. "Oh my god, T, why did you have to bring your infant with you?"

Twee turned red-faced, as if she was about to cry. Peebo started down the stairs to get the truck.

T sank against the fire extinguisher mounted to the wall and sighed. It had been a long night—longer than usual. "We don't do damage," T explained to Twee gently. "And if we leave the door open, someone else could *really* rob the place, or something worse."

"Just go back and close the door already," Vas said. "Problem solved, all right?"

"No," Kohl said. "*That*." She jog-walked out of the stairwell and down the corridor, pointing as she went. The fluorescent hallway lights buzzed and flickered. Sitting primly on the doormat in front of the open apartment door was a fluffy, red-collared cat.

"Unbelievable," Vas said. He put the blender down just inside the stairwell, leaned against the door to keep it from slamming closed and narrowed his eyes to watch. T froze—Twee did, too—as if even breathing might trip an alarm or cause someone to open their door in a panic.

"Kit-kit," Kohl whispered. She crouched and held out her hand to the cat, inching forward. The cat seemed pretty smart, for a cat, because it was clearly onto Kohl's trick and didn't trust her for anything. Just as Kohl lunged forward to grab it, the cat leapt sideways and went tearing down the corridor toward the rest of them; its nails made a rip-scrub sound on the carpet.

"Shit," Kohl hissed, scrabbling up.

"I got it!" Twee shouted. She pulled the fire door closed and dove heroically in the cat's direction.

"For crap's sake, *be quiet!*" Vas growled, rubbing his arm where Twee had shoved him. "Watch out. She's tiny, but she's dangerous," he growled when they all came back out into the hall to watch.

Once more, the cat bounded sideways. T dove, too, and then Vas, but the cat just ping-ponged between them and turned tail, tearing back down the hallway in a white streak. Kohl made one last valiant lunge as the cat scrambled toward her and she almost had him, but he swiped and hissed, kicked sideways, and disappeared through the apartment's open door. Kohl grabbed the door and pulled it closed, then slumped against it to breathe.

"Oh my god!" Twee called, running toward Kohl. "I am *so* sorry!"

Somewhere down the hallway, a lock clicked. Someone had heard them.

"Get!" Vas grunted through gritted teeth and slid into the stairwell. T held the door, dancing from foot to foot as Kohl thundered down the hall, whispering *shitshitshitshit*.

"I'm sorry," Twee cried. "I'm sorry; I'm sorry!"

Kohl made it to the fire door and shoved Twee into the stairwell, then hustled after her. T swung in behind them and let the door click shut.

"I'm sorry!" Twee moaned again, but Kohl grabbed her wrist and jerked her toward the stairs.

"No time!" she said over her shoulder.

"It's okay," T breathed. "You just have to be careful."

The four of them rumbled down the metal stairs and through the lobby. They banged through the front doors and onto the sidewalk just as Peebo pulled up in the pickup. T pulled Twee into the flatbed. The rest of them piled into the truck cab in a mess of limbs and grunts, and then Peebo took off.

T BANGED ON THE CAB's rear window until Kohl opened it. Nobody said anything, but it didn't matter—T just wanted to feel a little connected to the rest of them. They silently rocked and bumped with the traffic. Then Vas hit the dashboard.

"What was that back there?" he asked. "Besides a royal shit show?"

By the time they'd all gotten to the truck, it had started raining, as it seemed to do in Pittsburgh whenever it wasn't snowing or steaming with humid sun. When they started moving, it got worse, so T took the piece of cardboard they kept in the flatbed and held it up as a shield. It wouldn't be bad unless it really started to pour. Peebo sat stone-stiff and drove mechanically, braking and easing forward with the rhythm of the stoplights. The wipers dragged loudly across the windshield.

"I'm sorry," Twee said meekly into the little rear window, speaking directly to the back of Vas's head. She'd said it so much lately, it just sounded like a jumble of syllables. Peebo glared at Twee in the rearview mirror.

"Should've just left the cat."

"Are you kidding me?" Kohl said.

"It was indoors. Someone would have found it," Peebo said.

Kohl reached across Vas and punched Peebo's knee.

"Quit it." Peebo knocked her hand away.

Kohl punched one more time, then opened her window and stuck her face into the rain's splatter. T reached into the cab and put a hand on her back, but Kohl shrugged it off. "Exchange one for one, take nothing else, do no damage," she intoned.

"What is *that*?" Vas said. Twee was clutching a bundle of matted fur. "Did you take the *cat*?"

"It's just a thing." Twee held up a little stuffed monkey, one of the windup ones with the cymbals and the little red cap. She waggled it. "He's cute."

Kohl whipped around to stare at Twee. "Did you take that? From the house?"

"He needs a better home, with better people."

"Not okay," Kohl said.

"It's a lucky monkey. We need some luck. I'm thinking band mascot."

"You're not even *in* the band! That monkey could probably contribute more to the band than you can. At least it plays an instrument."

Vas grabbed the monkey out of Twee's hands and wound it up. The monkey whirred, then jerkily mashed its cymbals together a few times. It made a pitiful plastic clapping noise, not like cymbals at all.

"We're keeping it. Plays better than Peebo."

"Let's see him play the drums, though," Peebo said. It was an uncharacteristically good-humored response.

"The Dispossessed could use some luck. And some rhythm," Vas said.

Twee looked hopefully at T and Kohl. T sighed and shrugged. Kohl looked furious.

"Majority wins!" Twee shouted gleefully.

"We're not a democracy. We're better than that." Kohl glared at Twee. "At least, we *were*."

Kohl leaned back in her seat and closed her eyes. Peebo pressed the truck through the rain. There was a hole in the floor in front of the passenger seat and, even though they'd covered it up with a mat so road stones wouldn't bounce up and blind anybody, it didn't stop the noise. They all sat in silence, listening to the wet hiss of the street and grinding rumble of tires against the pavement. Vas set the monkey on the dashboard and wound him up. The monkey did its jerky cymbal-mashing.

When Peebo took the next corner, he sped up and yanked the wheel extra hard. Everybody wobbled sideways. The monkey fell off the dash and onto the floor, still going *dunt-dunt-dunt* with the plastic cymbals.

Kohl glared toward the whirring toy. "First the cat, now the monkey. It's so simple. Rule one: Do no damage."

"Right," Vas said. "No damage. Except breaking into their house, taking their stuff, and making them feel unsafe. But no damage." He rolled his eyes.

"It's a political statement," Twee said.

T nudged her shoulder and tried to give a warning look.

"What?" Twee said.

Peebo pulled the truck to a sudden stop and twisted around in his seat. Traffic zipped by, horns blaring. "What would you even know about it? You've been here for, like, five minutes!" he shouted.

"And anyway, you almost got us caught!" Vas chimed in.

The lights of passing cars flashed and blurred on the rainy pavement. Peebo hit the steering wheel and started the truck forward.

"Chicks, man," Vas said.

"What the hell?" Kohl said.

"Don't take it personally," Vas sneered. "I'm just saying what we all think."

"Not me," T said.

"You're on your own here, man," Peebo said to Vas, and T smiled a tight, bitter smile.

"It's not a *statement*. It's an *act*," Kohl said into the open window. "It's a political *action*."

"What's the difference, even?" Twee asked petulantly.

"Oh my god, here we go," Vas said.

"Honey, no," T said to Twee, and tried to lean in between Twee and Kohl. The whole argument was ridiculous and it wasn't about politics. T didn't care about the politics the way Vas and Kohl did—Peebo probably didn't care much either. Being together was so much better than being alone—T and Peebo knew that from experience. T figured

Vas and Kohl were probably just scared, and they used the politics to cover it up. But it wasn't wise to start something over politics—everything was so tenuous to begin with, even someone as small as Twee could easily rock the boat and tip it over.

Kohl turned completely around in her seat to stare at Twee. "Who *are* you?"

"Oh, your face!" Twee cried, reaching through the cab window toward the bright red scratch across Kohl's cheek.

"Don't," Kohl said, shifting away. "Hurts." She put two fingers against the scratch protectively.

"What happened?" T asked.

"Damn cat got me," Kohl said. "You try to be nice and this is what you get." She stuck her face back out the window as best she could from behind Peebo's seat.

When Twee whimpered and apologized again, Kohl nodded solemnly and said, "It's fine. It's really fine."

THE NEXT DAY, KOHL TIED a scarf around the shaved part of her head, tried to rub the scuffs off her ballet flats, and left the squat before anyone else was up. When she returned in the afternoon, she victoriously tossed a garment bag across the pile of coats and milk crates, clunked a bag full of containers of Cup Noodles on the counter, and handed a napkin-wrapped doughnut to T.

"Occasion?" T asked, scooping out some of the pink jelly filling with a finger.

"Job!" she beamed, then let her face fall. "It's for a *magician*, though."

"What?" Peebo perked up amongst the milk crates where he'd been napping. He pushed the garment bag off his knees, then seemed to really see it and held it up. "What's this?"

"I got a job. As an assistant. To The Stupendous Kevin. Who is a magician," Kohl enunciated slowly as if she was speaking to a child. It *was* Peebo, after all. "For four dollars an hour. Which is money. Money buys *food*." She tapped the noodle cups emphatically.

"Oh my god!" T danced her in a circle. "Magician money is still green, isn't it?"

"He advanced me twenty dollars, so I'll be working for free for a bit."

"I see bread in our future!" T said.

"Cigarettes," Peebo added.

"What is *that*?" T asked, poking the garment bag.

"It's pretty gross."

"What is?" T prompted. "Did you steal something?"

Kohl sighed, took the garment bag to the counter, then slid the vinyl bag up over the hanger to reveal what had to be the ugliest outfit any of them had ever seen. It was a hot pink bodysuit fitted with a shiny, orange lamé miniskirt and so many sequins and beads that it actually rattled when she picked it up.

"Sparkly," Peebo said.

"It's not so bad," T said.

"Wait," Kohl said, and disappeared into T's tent. She emerged after a moment, bare-legged, bare-armed, and virtually stuffed into the suit. Her breasts spilled over the top and jiggled like undercooked eggs.

"It's not so bad," T repeated blankly. Kohl put her hands on her hips and rolled her eyes.

"It's not so good, either," Peebo laughed.

"I know," Kohl said.

"Bazooms," T said.

"I know." Kohl smacked her overflowing flesh. When she moved, the sequins caught the light and hurled it back.

"Ow, my eyes," Peebo said.

THE STUPENDOUS KEVIN TURNED OUT to be a pretty good boss. All Kohl had to do was wear the damn outfit and smile and gesture a lot and, once, get in a box, fold up her legs, and scream as though she were being sawed in half. It was a little bit like acting, she supposed, having to do ridiculous stuff and pretend it wasn't ridiculous.

It all would have been great if there were no actual gigs.

The first one was a miserable affair: a party for some four-year-old who seemed to have been dipped in cake frosting and never, not once, stopped screaming. Kohl tried to sparkle and look excited when one of the dads introduced The Stupendous Kevin and his Beautiful Assistant Jasmine, but it was a big strain and made her face muscles hurt to keep smiling.

The kids mostly ignored Kevin, and the parents seemed mostly interested in keeping the kids seated, herding them back to a spot on the floor whenever any of them went sneaking off to eat more cake or play with a thing (there were things to play with scattered everywhere). Kevin poofed and waved his cape, snapped flash papers, and tried to make everything look more exciting than it was. When he did the sawing-Kohl-in-half trick, Kohl tried to make it seem real. She struggled and screamed for help and made desperate faces.

The kids didn't seem to care one bit.

Afterward, the parents fringing the room clapped politely, and the kids shot up and out of the house, screaming and pushing each other and generally venting the sugar in their systems because the parents were, for once, letting them go unfettered.

When the kids were gone to the backyard, Kevin snapped to action, handing out his business cards to the lingering parents and trying to hint to the hostess that it was time to pay him. Kohl squatted, tossing silk scarves and plastic flowers and magical detritus into the rolling suitcase that held Kevin's props. None of the adults would look in her direction; Kohl figured the blinding sequins and her jiggling, popping-out flesh were probably too much for them to handle. Finally, after she'd been crawling around on the floor at their feet for several minutes, one of the dads—Kohl couldn't have said which dad, since they all seemed to look exactly alike—squatted next to her to help scoop up Kevin's leavings.

"Was this a good show or a bad one?" he said, winking at her.

"What?"

"Did this go how it usually goes, or were our kids exceptionally awful?" He looked at her sheepishly. "We should have done the cake after, probably. They couldn't sit still."

"Dunno," Kohl said. "First time."

"Seriously? You'd never know. You're great."

"Really." Kohl made it less a question than an irritated statement. She focused on scraping glitter off the floor and piling it onto a paper plate for the trash.

"We'll get that later with a vacuum," the guy said. "Don't worry about it at all. I'm Paul." He stuck out his hand. "You're Jasmine, right?"

"No. That's not my real name."

"Did you choose Jasmine because you want to be a princess?"

"I didn't choose it. It was given to me. By Kevin. It was actually a surprise to me today."

Kohl glanced at Paul's still-outstretched hand and then at her own hands, which were full of glitter; his hand dropped to his side. One of the kids outside had begun to scream bloody murder, and most of the parents in the room rushed out. Paul stayed where he was.

"What do you do when you're not being sawed in half?" he asked.

Kohl was clearly giving the guy nothing to go on, but he kept trying to drag the conversation along as if they were propped on a couch with International Coffees or something. There was nothing to do but respond, since she couldn't be outright rude while she was working. She rolled her eyes at him, though.

"I'm a student."

"Oh? What are you studying? Probably not magic, I assume." Paul winked again.

"Probably not."

"What, then? Science? I love a smart girl."

Kohl looked at him hard. His face was a little beefy, with a line of skin bumping up between his eyebrows as if he spent a lot of time furrowing them. Paul had practically no actual eyebrows, just the lumps of flesh where they should have been. What little hair he did have there was nearly colorless, so that it took on the red hue of his skin and almost disappeared.

"English lit major."

"Lit? That's unusual, isn't it?"

"It's one of the biggest majors at school," Kohl said blankly.

"Yeah, but didn't your parents try to make you study science or math?"

"Nope."

"I thought kids like you got forced into it."

Kohl looked around desperately, but Kevin was nowhere to be found. Nobody, in fact, was around. No rescue possible. No knight on a white horse coming for her. She could hear, out in the yard, the kid still wailing and several adults cooing and soothing. Kohl pushed a denim-covered armchair a few inches and scraped madly at the carpet underneath, trying to look busy pulling up glitter that wasn't there.

"Kids like me? Magician's assistants? Left-handed kids? Girls? Or do you mean Indian kids?"

"Well," Paul said. "Everyone I know says that happens."

Kohl looked up at him, finally. "You have a lot of Indian friends?"

"Well," Paul said again, which clearly meant "no," but he wasn't going to say that. To end the conversation, Kohl held up a glitter-covered palm like a sparkling stop sign. He sat quietly. Kohl could practically hear gears turning as he considered her.

"English major," he said. "Writing? Are you writing the great American novel?"

"No, reading."

"Like *Beowulf*?"

"No, twentieth century. *Beowulf* was late tenth century or something."

"You know your stuff."

"I learned that back in *high school*. Everybody did," Kohl said. She'd begun to rake the carpet so furiously she knocked against the armchair, and one of its pillows—cross-stitched with the word BLESSED and several hearts—came tumbling down between them. Paul replaced it on the chair seat. Kohl clenched her teeth.

Paul sighed, rocking onto his knees. He ducked to stick his face into Kohl's sightline, forcibly catching her eye. "Did I do something to tick you off? I'm just trying to be nice here."

"Your wife is probably ten feet away."

"My *ex*-wife is in Detroit."

"Look, I'm just trying to clean up," Kohl said. "It's my job."

"Right." Paul stood up. "Good luck. Thanks for a good show."

Kohl smiled weakly at him, because she knew she was supposed to smile unless the guy hit her or did some other violent thing. She felt bad for being a little rude and brushing him off like that when he hadn't done anything wrong, really. Parents were trickling back into the room, the kid's trauma apparently having been solved. Kohl finished shoving Kevin's junk into the suitcase and zipped it closed, then pulled her oversized sweatshirt over her head and down to cover her pillowing boobs and everything else to the knees. Kevin showed up right after there was nothing left to do.

"You okay? Was that guy bothering you?" He stood far too close for her comfort. Kohl figured that was so the parents shuffling around them couldn't hear, but it still felt gross. She backed up a step and dropped into one of the awful denim armchairs, then arched up to pull a plastic army guy from under her thigh.

"I'm fine. I can handle myself."

"Because I can step in if you ever need it." Kevin sniffed and leaned against the wall. He must've hit the light switch, because the lights went out and the hubbub stopped until he yelled, "Oops, sorry!" and flicked the lights back on.

"Yeah, thanks," Kohl said. "I'm fine. I took care of it myself. It's all good."

"Good show today. You did great," Kevin said. Kohl didn't respond, mostly because she was tired of having to talk when she didn't want to, but Kevin seemed to be waiting for her to speak, so she said, "You too."

"I thought so too! The flash paper really adds something, even though I'm not sure we should be using it in peoples' living rooms."

Kohl nodded; then, because Kevin still seemed to be waiting, she said, "The flash paper is great."

"Do you want to go get something to drink?" he asked. "I could use something after all these kids, and there's a pretty good place a couple blocks from here."

"I'm not exactly dressed for it," Kohl said, indicating her bare legs and the sequined tassels peeping out from beneath the sweatshirt.

"I can swing by your place so you can change," Kevin said hopefully.

"Thanks, Kevin, but I think I'm just going to go home and take a nap," Kohl said. She stood up and uselessly brushed the sweatshirt and the peeping tassels. "I have to write a paper later, and those kids fried my brain. Another time, okay?"

KEVIN DROVE KOHL BACK TO the squat and pulled over to let her out without turning off the engine. She was relieved he wasn't going to try to follow her. She got out of the car, then leaned into the open window.

"Thanks. Have a good night. Get some rest."

"Here," Kevin said, waving a white envelope in her direction. "Your part of the pay. We got a really good tip today."

Kohl took the envelope and tucked it into the pouch pocket of her sweatshirt. The sweatshirt had big maroon Gothic letters across the chest that read DUQUESNE UNIVERSITY OF THE HOLY SPIRIT. She'd gotten it at Goodwill, but she didn't mind people thinking she was a Duquesne girl. That meant they'd probably leave her alone. *Usually* it worked, she thought. Sometimes it only spurred them on, though.

"Here's some extra, too, for all the trouble," Kevin said, flopping a couple of five-dollar bills at her. Spurred, for sure.

"No, thanks, it's cool. Comes with the territory." She smiled and backed away from the car before Kevin could insist.

"Let's call it an asshole fee!" he called out the car window, still shaking the cash. Kohl laughed despite herself.

"It's fine!" she yelled back.

"Will I see you again?" Kevin asked.

"Of course." Kohl gave him an exasperated look. "If I still have a job, I'm there!" She turned and opened the lobby door, which she had left propped slightly open with a stick when she left so she didn't have to climb through the broken glass.

THANKS TO PEEBO'S HUSTLE, THE band got booked, finally. Tamale Mama's billed itself as a "Mexican-Themed Family Place," even though it was right smack in the middle of Forbes Avenue, near the O, a dirty, all-night French fry place frequented by drunk and stoned college kids. There were never any families at the O, or at Tamale Mama's, either—it was usually those same college kids looking for a cheap meal before they got themselves more drunk and more stoned. Still, everyone agreed, it was a real gig that paid real money and got a real—if paltry—audience.

They were supposed to play in the back while the sombreroed staff behind the counter served up "Tijuana Tacos" and "Por Favor Pork Sticks" in little paper boats on plastic trays to the rowdy, distracted crowd. The whole place smelled like vinegar and wet carpet.

"This sucks," Vas said.

"And blows." Kohl plugged her guitar into the beat-up Tamale Mama's amp. There were stickers from previous bands all over it. She ground at them with the toe of her shoe.

"This *pays*, you ingrates," Peebo said. He set the monkey toy on the floor next to the drum kit. It would have been great, but nobody was going to see it on the floor, behind the band's shoes. He wound it up anyway, and it bonked its cymbals.

A nervous-looking girl from the counter hustled to stand in front of the band. She nodded at them, then turned to face the tamale-eaters at their tables.

"Amigos," she said into the mic, while making a pained face. She said it like *Uh-me-goes*. T winced. "Amigos, please enjoy The Distraught!"

"It's Luckmonkey," T whispered.

"What?" the girl said into the mic. Her voice echoed too loudly over the restaurant's constant rumble of chewing and conversation.

Vas steered her out of the way, then held his arms out as if welcoming everybody to his castle.

"We're Luckmonkey, guys, and we're totally distraught to be here!"

THE AUDIENCE WASN'T INTO IT, not even a little bit. Most of them were more into ravaging their tamales and trying to shout above the music. People left. One guy yelled, "You suck!" The floor was littered with napkins and clumps of overcooked, rubbery masa.

Mostly, Luckmonkey kept going for the free tamales they were all supposed to get at the end, which were probably worth more than what they were getting paid.

Vas tried to wiggle sinuously on the mic like his hero Axl Rose, but T thought he just ended up looking as if he had an itchy crotch. When the group of freshman girls sitting near the counter started snickering and whispering, clearly about *him*, Vas lost it.

"'Star Fucker.' On three," he said, mostly to Peebo.

"No way, Vas," T said.

"We should do something *we* wrote," Vas argued.

"No way," T said again.

"Yeah, dude, this is a Family Place," Peebo said sarcastically, making air quotes with his drumsticks.

"One! Two! Three!" Vas shouted, and they all snapped into the song anyway, out of sheer habit. There was a longish intro that featured Kohl's mediocre guitar-playing while the rest of them clanged and plonked, speeding up and up as they always did, until the intro was over and Vas started to sing.

"Star fucker!" he shout-sang into the mic a few times in a sadly affected British accent. He sounded as if he was saying "stah fockah." It was pretty screwed up. "Star—"

Everything suddenly went tinny, and the manager stood in front of them, red-faced, holding the plug from the amp. He pushed his sombrero back so he could look Vas in the eye.

"Absolutely not!"

"C'mon man," Vas practically wheedled.

"This is a family place!"

Vas looked around dramatically and said, "*This?* Is a *family* place?"

Some kid in a frat jersey threw a handful of shredded iceberg lettuce at Vas. "It's a family place, dude!"

"It's full of college kids. Half of them are already drunk."

The manager put his foot on the amp, then leaned against his knee like a football coach. He had the same khaki pants and cruddy black sneakers, the same slicked-back hair, the same pudgy red hands all high school football coaches seemed to have. The only difference was the sombrero, as though he were a football coach in some weird, alternate universe full of stereotypes and bad hair.

"It's a family place. Family-owned, family-run. For families," he said as if talking to a child.

"I get it," Vas said. It was clear to T that he didn't get anything, because Vas didn't really believe in rules, especially rules about what polite people were supposed to do, but at least he was pretending to get it.

"You can sing 'star effer' next time," the manager suggested.

Vas snorted. "No way, man."

"What's the difference?" T asked reasonably. "Everybody's going to know that means 'fucker,' anyway."

"The difference…" The manager turned on T. "…is that it's not *language*. We cannot condone *language* at Tamale Mama's."

"What are you speaking right now?" Kohl mumbled and caught T's eye.

"This is worthless," Vas said. Peebo was already standing up and shoving the drumsticks into his back pocket. "We're leaving."

Kohl unplugged her guitar from the amp and slid it into its padded nylon bag. T stood, hands still poised on the guitar neck and strings, just in case they started playing again all of a sudden.

"No dice," the manager said. "If you leave, you don't get paid."

"I guess we don't get paid, then, because look at me leaving right now," Vas said. "Tamale Mama's supports censorship!" he shouted toward the crowd of diners, who barely paused shoving food in their mouths to look up. Vas stormed up the aisle of plastic tables toward the front door.

"Fascists!" he shouted. He picked up a tamale off the tray of a nearby drunk kid and shook it at him. "Taco fascists!" He raised his fist in the air as he left. The door jingled its bells cheerfully as he slammed out. Peebo saluted the paltry crowd, then hurried after him.

"That's a tamale! Learn the difference!" the manager shouted after Vas, which seemed like the saddest, most not-the-point thing to do.

"Let's go," Kohl said to T. "Pack up." She picked up her guitar case.

T grabbed the case to the guitar but didn't bother with it and simply slung the guitar over one shoulder before following Kohl onto the street.

CHAPTER 4

THE APPRENTICE

"We got turned down by Mason-Dixon Bar, The Stereo Stop, Wilkie's, even the *Eat'n Park*," Peebo moaned. He kicked the wall, and somehow his socked foot was dirty enough to leave a scuff like a grey scowl on the plaster.

Kohl sat on the floor next to Peebo and pulled his head into her lap. She cupped his cheeks.

"It's okay. We just need to try more places," she said, stroking Peebo's nose.

"*We* need to do that? I've been walking around the Pitts all day trying more places. My feet are wrecked. How about someone else does it for once?"

"Yeah, I'll do it tomorrow after work, when the bars open," she soothed. "We'll make it happen."

Peebo glared at her and knocked her hand off his face.

"Quit it, that itches. Plus, do you know what they're saying? What the guy at Eat'n Park told me?" He kicked the wall a couple more times, leaving more greasy scuffs. "We are *inappropriate* and therefore *unwelcome.* That damn Pitt-stain at Mama Taco's is telling everybody to avoid us."

"Tamale Mama's," T said.

"It's okay. We just gotta find better places," Kohl said.

"Inappropriate for Eat'n Park," Peebo snorted. "Who are they kidding? After ten, it's all drunk college kids barfing strawberry milkshakes into their French fries. But *we're* inappropriate."

"People are hypocrites," T said, shrugging.

Peebo sat up at that. "You of all people should know what a stupid thing that is to say," he hissed. "They're assholes. Racist. Classist. Scared by gays."

"Sexist," Kohl put in.

"All kinds of assholery," Peebo said.

"What do you mean, me 'of all people'?" T said, though it wasn't really a question.

"Because of the he-she thing."

"The *what*?"

"You know what I mean," Peebo said.

Kohl suddenly stood up, letting Peebo's head crack onto the floor.

"I'm done here," she said, while Peebo rubbed his head and mouthed, *ow, bitch*. She stomped away a few paces, then stomped back to glare at Peebo. "Why do you care what T chooses to be? If T or anybody else wants to be a boy, a girl, a whole wheat cracker, whatever, it's not your business; you *respect* that!"

"A whole wheat cracker?" T said.

From the tent, they heard Twee giggle. Everyone had forgotten she was there and, for a moment, they all stopped and stared at the blanket. Twee went silent, then said, "Sorry. I'm sorry."

"You know what I mean," Kohl snapped at T.

"I can fight my own battles. I can speak for myself," T said.

"Then why *don't* you?" Kohl yelled.

When T spoke, it was almost inaudible, heavy and level. "Because I'm getting tired of battles all the damn time, and it's not a war I'm going to win, and sometimes I just want to sit there and be angry and not be waved around like a flag for everybody else's territory fight." T crawled into the blanket-tent and straight into bed, pushed the blanket edges closed with an anticlimactic *whiff,* and shook off Twee's gentle touch when she offered it. From inside the tent, T yelled, "And it's not, for the billionth time, a *choice!*"

"Don't attack *me*," Kohl yelled back. "I'm trying to *defend* you! I don't have to do that, you know!"

T appeared to be punching the blanket, because the material shimmied and bellied out to punctuate T's words. "No, you don't. I guess it's your *choice!*"

"Wow," said Kohl. She grabbed the pack of cigarettes, shook one out and left, slamming the door behind her.

"Nice work," Peebo said to the blanket. He crammed his feet into his sneakers without messing with the laces, picked up the cigarette pack from the floor where Kohl had thrown it, and shoved a cigarette in his mouth. "Your nitpicking has alienated the only two people in the world who were willing to put up with you."

"I'm willing," Twee said hoarsely, but Peebo didn't seem to hear her at all. "Enjoy the silence, *dude*," he said as he left, letting the door jitter open and gape after him.

Dear homeowner:

Congratulations! Your possession has been Uprooted.

Do not be alarmed: you have not been robbed, nothing has been damaged and no one has been harmed; your   naked guy statue   has simply been repossessed by the universe… To compensate for the loss you probably feel, the universe has left you this very nice   blender . Please enjoy!

—*The Uproots*

THEY WERE ALMOST OUT. *ALMOST.* T put the blender and note on the kitchen counter. It looked a little weird, the bright silver blender like a Corvette in the gingham-and-polished-oak country kitchen (who were they fooling with that kitchen in a *high-rise apartment in downtown Pittsburgh*, really?), but it was a pretty nice blender, so T tried not to feel too bad about it. Peebo and Vas wrapped a slender wood statuette like a gift bottle in a couple discarded paper shopping bags while Kohl watched and Twee whispered endlessly, like a nervous river, "Hurry, hurry, hurry, you guys, I hear something someone's coming, hurry up!"

They were almost out, but then a kid showed up.

When a key started scratching in the front door lock, Twee really got going, more plaintively repeating *you guys, you guys!* And then the door popped open and a boy—probably about sixteen, with moppy brown hair and pants that sagged as though they were full of wrenches or rocks or stolen electronics, or whatever the kids were packing these days—a sloppy, mopey, uncareful boy shuffled in.

It took a minute, during which everybody froze and held their breath, before the boy looked up and noticed them. Then he froze too.

"What," he said like a statement.

"Don't worry," Kohl said, holding up her hands. "It's okay."

The boy, as unkempt as he looked, as ill-fitting and threadbare as his clothes were, radiated money the way dressed-down rich people always look rich. "Who are you guys? Did my dad hire you?"

"Well," Kohl said, still holding up her hands. Beside her, Twee had gone pale and very, very still.

"Is my dad home already?"

"Dude, use your head," Vas said over his shoulder. He stood up with the paper-wrapped statuette shoved under his arm. "We're robbing you."

The kid's eyes widened, but, to his credit, he maintained his cool. "If you're taking me as a hostage, can I at least change my clothes first?"

"What?" Kohl said. "No hostages. No guns. We're not *robbing* you. We're switching possessions." She looked emphatically at Vas. "We take one thing and leave one thing."

Vas sighed. "We're taking your thing, but we left you a different thing. It's a thing we do, a whole political *thing*."

"Are you taking my dad's fake fertility statue?" The kid looked excited.

"Well," Kohl said, at the same time that Vas happily rapped the top of the paper-wrapped statue and said, "Yep!"

Kohl glared at him and shook her head.

"Awesome," the kid said. "I hate that thing. Did you notice the big dong? Of course you did. How do you not notice it?"

Peebo and Vas both looked intrigued. They'd been so busy wrapping it they hadn't looked at what it *was* or considered what the foot-long needle-like protrusion might be, other than thinking that it made wrapping a difficult project and that somebody was bound to get skewered.

But Peebo said, "Of course," anyway.

"What's the political thing?"

Vas opened his mouth, but Kohl interrupted, waving toward the kitchen. "There's a note where we explain it all in there." Then she looked at Peebo and T and said, "C'mon, we gotta go."

"Can I come?" the kid asked.

"What?" T said.

"I wanna join."

Peebo thumped the kid on the back. He actually looked bigger than usual, as if he'd suddenly gained fifty pounds and grown six inches.

"It's not a club," T said, gently pushing the kid out of the way to get to the door.

"I get it, though," the kid wheedled.

"Keep on," Twee said, holding up a fist as she marched out the door. T patted the kid on the shoulder before slipping out after her, saying, "We can't take you, kid. Sorry about it."

The kid looked pissed off. Kohl closed the door before he could follow them. *Sorry,* she mouthed as she did.

From behind the door, the kid yelled, "What'd we get, at least?"

THEY MADE IT BACK TO the squat without dying, which was truly lucky since Peebo drove like a lunatic the whole way back, stomping on the gas to fly through red lights and squealing the truck around corners. He parallel parked at the curb, ramming the cars in front of and behind him several times each as he did. When he got out and slammed the door, the chrome handle fell off and rolled under the tire.

"Just perfect," Peebo said, bending down to search for the handle in the gutter. Then he stood up and kicked the door. "Forget it. Piece of crap."

"It seems like you're always ticked off," Twee said.

Peebo, ignoring her, stormed up the stairs to the squat.

ONCE THEY ALL MADE IT back, Vas closed the door and set the statue on its back on the counter. The protrusion poked up like a finger pointing accusingly at the ceiling. Twee curled up on the mess of milk crates and coats, and T sat beside her.

"That was exhausting," Twee said. "I'm completely wiped from being so freaked out. How do you guys do that all the time?"

"It's not usually like that," T said.

Kohl violently kicked off her shoes, letting them skitter across the floor until they thumped the wall. "We've never been caught," she said. "Until you showed up."

"It's not Twee's fault," T said. "We couldn't have predicted that kid would show up."

"Lotta good this piece of junk did us," Kohl said, tossing the monkey statue on the pile of milk crates. It clipped Twee in the hip before tumbling a few times and landing on its side against the wall.

"Control yourself. You're acting like a spoiled brat," T said, but Kohl sulked against the counter, ignoring T.

Peebo scrabbled in the cigarette carton for a smoke but gave up before he got one. Instead, he crouched near the door and wrapped his bony arms around his bony knees. He looked tired. "At least somebody knows about us now."

"What's that mean?" T asked.

"I *mean*," Peebo said, pausing to sigh dramatically, "we're not changing anything. Nobody cares what we're doing. We've never even been mentioned on the news. We're not even making a dent."

"That's not true," Kohl said. "We're changing things."

"Really?" Peebo said, shooting her a look.

"I think so," Kohl said.

"I don't see it." Peebo shook his head. "We do this, and we do this, and we do this, and we do this, and *still* we have to do this *again* because not one piece of crap *ever changes*. People are still hungry. And homeless. And needy. And those assholes keep buying their exercise bikes and their vintage watches and they're still voting for Greedy Rich Guy #67, and they're still walking right by when someone asks for help like they *don't even notice.*"

T said, "It's not the kind of thing you're going to see. It's not instant gratification."

Twee was, for once, quietly hanging back, watching them argue. She seemed to be building her silence into a *moment,* but, when the argument slacked enough for her to speak, all she said was, "Nobody ever notices me, but I still get in my cage. You *have* to."

Everyone looked at her as if they'd just remembered she was there.

"No, you don't. You can do something *better*," Vas said.

"Tell me what that is," Kohl said.

Twee was clearly going to speak again—her face had that *look,* as if she were trying to be the first person to answer a teacher's question. T wrapped both arms around her shoulders and steered her into the tent, whispering *not now, not now* in her ear.

Inside the tent, T pretended not to listen to the angry voices outside and pulled Twee down to sit on the floor. The sounds of Peebo, Vas and Kohl arguing weren't muffled much. T thought about kissing Twee, just for distraction, but then Peebo yelled over the rumbling of the other voices, "How the hell are we supposed to spread the message if we turn away anyone willing to listen?"

"We took *her* on and look at *that* mistake!"

It was Kohl who yelled it, but the silence afterward seemed to indicate that they all agreed. T looked at Twee, whose eyes widened and went watery.

"Learning curve. It's okay," T said, touching Twee's face lightly.

Twee shook her head and let it drop to her knees; she folded up so small T could have fit her in an overnight bag.

"You know what?" Vas shouted.

T heard the door slam, just as Kohl shouted, "No, wait!"

Peebo said nothing at all.

CHAPTER 5

TO GET RID OF THE GUN,
YOU HAVE TO PICK UP THE GUN

AFTER EVERYONE HAD SLEPT POORLY, gone out for the day, and come home again, T and Twee concocted another horrible mess of food (lumpy, snot-colored, unappetizing). The four of them sat silently, busy with anything but talking about the Vas-shaped hole in the room for an hour. Twee was braiding scraps of fabric into a long strip, which she said she'd use to make a rug. T wiped the dishes with a sheet of newspaper. Peebo scribbled doodles on the wall with a ballpoint pen; the tip made a quiet *whir-snick-whir* as he drew.

Suddenly, Kohl slapped a wad of dollar bills on the counter and said, "I'm keeping ten, but the rest is for the group."

They all stared at the crumpled money; there had to be at least fifty dollars.

"Where'd you get that?" Twee asked.

"I sold my guitar to a Pitt student wannabe rocker."

"You what?" T practically shouted. "You love that thing!"

"I also like to eat food and have soap," Kohl said with a sad smile. "Life is choices, at least for most of us. Except rich people. They never have to make choices. I guess that's the thing."

Peebo was already leaning back into the pile of coats he used as a sofa bed whenever he wanted to stretch out. "What about Luckmonkey?"

"The band or the toy? I have no idea where the toy went. The band is clearly dead. We can't get a gig thanks to Vas's tantrum."

There was a moment of silence because, even though every single one of them knew it was true, and selling the guitar was probably necessary since they didn't bring in that much money by other means, it was a shock to hear someone say out loud that the band was done.

"Who's going to tell Vas?"

"If he comes back, you mean."

"He'll be back," Peebo said. "He needs this place as much as we do. Plus, we still have The Uproots to do."

Peebo found the stuffed monkey mixed in with the coats and pulled it out to fidget with it. When Kohl saw it, she said, "For god's sake, it's like herpes," and when T looked at her curiously, she said, "Every time you hope it's gone for good, it comes back again."

Peebo rested the monkey against his caved-in belly, wound it up, and let it bash its cymbals together. They all watched it; the only sound was its dull clapping and pitiful mechanical whir. Eventually, the whir began to drag, and the cymbal claps syncopated to a stop. The monkey froze with its cymbals pulled wide apart and its head thrown back at the top end of a nod.

WHEN THE FRONT DOOR POPPED open, Peebo jerked around to see what was happening—they all did, because it had been so quiet between them and then the creak and bang of the door suddenly wrecked it.

There was Vas. He had a gun.

Not pointed at anyone, not like that, but he came in carrying it like a hot potato and set it gently on the coats piled on the milk crates near the door. He carefully aimed it at the wall, but everybody still moved well away. Kohl moved so fast the pile of work in front of her slipped over, leaving books and papers splayed across the floor. She didn't even notice.

"What the hell is that?" she asked, which was a pointless question, since they all knew exactly what it was.

"Where did that come from?" T asked at the same time.

Vas looked at them all calmly and said, "I got it off a guy at work. It's a loaner."

"It's a gun," Kohl said. She was shaking. "Get rid of it, Vas."

"File off the serial number," Peebo said. "Scratch it off with a knife."

It took T a moment to realize the rattling, banging noise was Kohl kicking the lower kitchen cabinet door with her heel. It got louder and faster until she seemed to explode.

"Get rid of it! Or get out! I don't want that anywhere near me." Kohl's hands were almost white, she was gripping the counter's edge so hard.

"Sometimes if you want to get rid of the gun, you have to pick the gun up," Vas said.

"What?"

"If you want to get rid of the gun, you have to pick it up," Vas repeated. "Huey Newton."

Twee had entirely disappeared from the room, and there was a noticeable empty space when she would have piped up and said something that pissed off half the room. Instead, T said, "Huey Newton was talking about a whole different situation."

Vas looked long and hard at all of them, then said, "Was he *really*?"

At that point, T had too many things to say, and so said nothing at all. Kohl stared pointedly at each of them in turn and shook her head, then shoved her feet into her shoes and left. The sound of the door closing behind her—not a slam, but a firm click—seemed louder than it was.

"I guess it's the thing to do, storming out," Peebo said. He made finger guns at T and Vas, then shut himself in the bathroom. They heard the pipes shudder and the shower groan to life.

Vas yelled, "No more than two minutes, seriously!" at the bathroom door.

"Or what, you'll shoot him?" T said.

"Shut up."

Crouching to crawl into the tent like some kind of scared dog was humiliating after all that, but T did it anyway. Twee was kneeling, trying to cram her extra T-shirt and shorts into the hip pocket of her jumper.

They spilled out and over the pocket's edge and the bulk of them pulled her dress funny, as if she were a burst sofa cushion. Her eyes were red.

"I can't stay here," she said before T had a chance to say anything.

"I wish you would."

"It's not safe here. I can't be near a gun."

"We're going to make Vas get rid of it. Nobody wants it here."

"Peebo's more fine with the gun being here than with me being here. And I think it's a toss-up for Kohl."

T couldn't say anything except "I wish you'd stay" again, so Twee crawled out of the tent without a word. T heard her mutter, "Bye, Vas," but didn't hear anything else, not even the door opening and closing when she left.

WHAT CHEKHOV SAID ABOUT A gun—that if it appears in the first act it should be fired in the second—worried T like a bad omen. Vas's gun became an un-dropped shoe. Vas insisted on bringing it when they went out that night, but it stayed tucked in his back pocket, where it stuck out awkwardly and made him walk with a jaunty bop.

They drove to Shadyside and chose a castle-looking place with blue wood siding and shingled turrets. Peebo shoved the lucky monkey figurine onto the dashboard, as if it could guard the car, then hopped out and sprinted across the lawn, bouncing in long leaps on his pipe-cleaner legs. He pried open one of the back windows, and they all skittered out of the van and squeezed into the house, getting streaks from rotten wood and flaking blue paint on their shirts as they went.

Vas, Peebo, T and Kohl tumbled onto a sloping, overstuffed velvet couch. The living room was dark, and, though there was a lot of space, there wasn't much to fill it. The floor was cement, painted in colored mandalas, chipped in as many places as it wasn't. Two wooden bookshelves creaked with books and papers, which were shoved haphazardly on the shelves and piled into teetering towers on top. There was little more: a rug, a ratty green blanket on the windowsill, and a collection of black and white photographs grouped tightly on one wall. Other than that, the room was almost bare.

"What can we even take here?" Kohl asked. "Everything seems precious."

"What about this atrocity?" Vas said, poking the one useless thing in the room, a plastic Pittsburgh Pirates figurine in full baseball gear with an exaggeratedly large bobbling head. He poked it again, and the baseball guy grinned and nodded, grinned and nodded.

"It's probably sentimental," Kohl said. "I mean, why else would you keep that thing?"

"There's no possession problem here. We take nothing." T had already started toward the door.

"We should check the other rooms, at least," Vas said, jiggling the handle of the one enormous Dutch door at the room's end. The top half of it popped open, while the bottom half stayed closed.

"Whoa," Vas said, his head stuck through the top opening of the door. "Come and look. What is this?"

On the other side of the door was a kitchen. At least, it looked as though it used to be a kitchen. Now there was no stove, no refrigerator, no chairs or table, no curtains on the greasy window above the sink. The floor was the same polished concrete as the living room. A bag of dry dog kibble was pushed to the back of the counter, and in front of it withered a paltry stack of carrots. A paper fast food cup with a chewed, limp straw had been placed on the edge of the sink.

"We should go. There's nothing," Peebo said.

"We should leave them the statue, at least, so they can sell it," said Kohl.

They heard, then, the scratch of claws on wood and a growl that revved into barking. Vas jumped back just before a huge dog, all hot breath and stringing saliva, slapped its front paws on the top of the lower door and snapped its yellow teeth at them. The door rattled, and the dog's nails scraped against it in what appeared to be a desperate attempt to launch over it into the living room.

Vas had drawn the gun before he—or anyone—knew what was happening. He stood a few feet from the door with gun aimed at the dog's quivering pink face, but the dog continued to bark.

"Put that thing down," Kohl hissed at Vas.

"I'm not shooting a dog," he said, "unless it comes at me first."

"No, the *gun,* put the *gun* down. Jeez."

"It's blind," said T. Then, because Vas made a weird face, T said, "The *dog,* not the *gun.*"

It appeared to be true: The dog was nearly entirely white, squat and muscular, and it seemed to be barking without seeing them. Its eyes were milky blue. Drool spilled over its slack gums, and it smelled terrible. Vas tucked the gun back into his pants and backed away in several large steps.

"We need to leave," T said. "If anyone's home, we're dead."

Peebo shuffled backward toward the window through which they'd entered until Vas said, "We might as well use the front door."

Kohl yanked open the door and the four of them tripped toward the truck. It wasn't until they were all safely packed into it that they realized they'd set the house alarm blaring. And they'd kept the fertility statue, still in its paper bag wrapper.

There wasn't time to take it back into the house, and, between the dog's barking and the alarm wailing, there was too much noise to think straight. Peebo slammed the truck into gear and peeled out.

IT WAS UGLY: KOHL TOLD Vas that if he intended to keep the gun, he'd have to move out of the squat. Vas said she was being a chickenshit fascist, and Kohl said fascists tended to love their guns. T said the gun was ridiculous because it was dangerous and unnecessary. Vas disagreed, but not even Peebo liked the gun much, even though he thought it was probably necessary. Everyone yelled and arm-waved and stormed around. The gun sat on the counter between them all, insistent as an accusation.

"We are nonviolent. That means we reject even the *option* of violence," Kohl yelled.

"That gets us nowhere," Vas said levelly. "We might as well use the only language people understand nowadays."

"And just exactly what would we be saying in that language?"

"That this can't continue. That rich people are selfish and cruel and they can't be allowed to do what they're doing to the rest of us."

"They have to reorganize their values," Peebo added. "They can't be smug. They're not as safe as they think they are."

"If we can't *all* be safe, then *none* of us are safe," Vas said.

They all seemed to agree with that; *it's just the* how *of it all that's in question*, T thought. For such a heated argument, it was strangely calm, with the four of them leaning close over the counter at which T and Kohl had spent so much time cooking. Their faces now were so close they practically touched. Kohl clenched T's thigh under the counter. Peebo scratched at a dried splotch of something stuck to the surface. Vas's breath wafted a sour smell. All of it turned T's stomach.

"What happened to the project? The Uproots? To teaching all that by redistributing their stuff?" Kohl asked.

"It's not working anymore," Peebo said. "If it ever did."

"This," Vas said, patting the gun, "is a very loud voice." Vas's hand on the gun made the argument feel uneven and dangerous.

"It's not a very *clear* voice," Kohl said.

"We need to take some sort of stand," Vas said.

That seemed to T to be exactly the problem, standing firmly in one place. That got you knocked down as often as it didn't. Even tall buildings were built to sway a bit so they didn't fall over so easily. *Float like a butterfly*, T thought, but the gun was a pin, a heavy fist, an anvil. It anchored everything in the room around it.

"Who's 'we,' rich boy?" Kohl said.

"This isn't the right stand," T said, but not, apparently, out loud.

While everyone else continued to shout, T pulled open the tent flap and crawled inside to muffle the entire argument with a pillow.

The light in the tent was colored pink; the filter of the pillow turned it gray and dark and quiet enough to sleep.

IT WAS THE MIDDLE OF the night, the light entirely gone, when the loud crack broke T's sleep. It was as if a truck had crashed into the building: a slam of metal, shouting and noises outside the tent like things being knocked over, everything breaking, and T on the sleeping bag on the floor, still trying to shake back into consciousness.

When T got some sense, whipped open the makeshift tent and scrambled out, the squat had gone still. The air smelled like campfire. Kohl was crouched against the wall, crying, hands stuffed between her thighs. Peebo knelt next to her, hand on her back. Vas bent over them both, and he was actually crying, too, saying *fuckfuckfuckfuck* and trying to pry Kohl's hands free with his shaking fingers.

"Everyone's fine," Peebo said, holding up his hand to slow T's panic. He went back to stroking Kohl's hair.

"Just let me see, Kohl," Vas said. His voice wavered strangely.

"Stings, but it's fine. It's fine."

"What happened?" T came to crouch next to them. "I fell asleep."

At that, Kohl's tears renewed, and she began to sob outright. Peebo put his arm protectively around her shoulders.

"Gun went off," Peebo said. "Everybody's fine."

Kohl gave him a red-eyed dirty look, but Peebo for once said nothing back.

"How the hell did the gun go off?" T said.

Peebo looked at T, trying for a significant glare to shut the whole thing down. "We'll talk about it later."

"I grabbed it. It was my fault. I was going to throw it out the window. I set it off," Kohl babbled.

Peebo sighed. He pointed to the far wall, where a tiny hole still fumed, spilling crumbling plaster.

"Kohl tried to pick up the gun, and it went off. Hit the wall. Nobody got hurt—"

"My ass! Seriously?" Kohl yelled. The side of her face was puffed up and red. There was a small place where it looked as though the skin had been scraped off. It wasn't bleeding, but it was raw and awful-looking.

"Kickback. Smacked her in the face when it fired. Nobody got *shot*."

Vas picked up the gun and carefully emptied out the rest of the bullets. He set it down on the floor again until Kohl started to scream.

"Get that the hell away from me! Get it *out*!"

"It's fine, it's empty, it can't do any damage."

Kohl lifted her head to stare at Vas. She looked wild; what unshaved hair she had was matted and stuck in clumps to her wet cheeks. "I don't care. I thought it was off before, and it blew up. Get it *out*."

"You can't turn a gun on or off," Vas said, but picked it up gingerly anyway and put it on the top of the nearest cupboard.

"Are you okay?" T asked.

"She's just scared," Peebo said gently, combing Kohl's hair back with his fingers.

"Stop it!" Kohl knocked his hand away and stood. "I'm fine. I'm just *pissed*. I got *hurt*. Someone could have been killed, and it would have been *my fault*." She burst into fresh tears. "And now I'm crying, and you're all treating me like some fragile *little girl*."

"We're all upset," Peebo said. "It's just that you're the one who got hurt."

"I'm fine," Kohl said.

"Peebo's crying, too. It's not because you're a girl," T said.

Peebo shot T a dirty look, but it was true. His eyes were red and watery and sore-looking. His lips were swollen. He looked as if he was biting down hard on his own tongue. T nodded to Peebo and steered Kohl toward the tent.

"Here," T said. "Come lie down with me."

"Try to sleep it off," Peebo said, at which Kohl laughed bitterly; but she let T steer her into the tent.

T gently, gently slipped Kohl out of her clothes. She went limp and let T drag the fabric off of her until she was sitting nearly naked on the sleeping bag. "Come on, now," T said, and slipped a fresh T-shirt over her head. T pressed her backwards until she was lying down, then enclosed her in a cocoon of arms and legs and pressed her face against T's chest, figuring a calm heartbeat would work to slow her own, as it did with babies.

"I don't want that gun here," Kohl said, hiccupping. "I never did. It's gone, or I am."

"We'll take care of it in the morning. I promise."

T squeezed her a little, then leaned back so she could have most of the pillow. Kohl snuffled and whispered, "*Fine.*" Her breath stuttered in a couple sobs, then deepened and evened out until she was asleep.

It took T much longer to fall asleep. Afraid to disturb Kohl, T didn't move, but lay listening to Vas and Pcebo argue late into the night. T couldn't make out what they were saying; their voices were a hissing rumble, as if they were barely restrained from shouting. The noise rose and fell in violent contrapunto, background music that faded in and out of T's ears until there was nothing but exhausted sleep.

WHEN T WOKE, THE TENT was empty, and the squat was silent. Peebo crouched on the pile of coats and milk crates, cupping a bodega coffee to his chest.

"Where is everybody?" T asked.

"Kohl went to work with that Stupid Kevin guy. They have a birthday party in Mount Washington. Vas left. He's returning the gun."

THE WALK ALONG THE RIVER was a relief after the humming dry heat of the laundromat. T walked up and down the water's edge twice, but there was no sign of Twee or her dog cage. Groups of partying kids leaned on the park benches, leaned on the stone walls, leaned against each other, making out and tipping half-hidden beer cans to their mouths. Dusk began to close in on the promenade. Fireflies lit the air in tiny, singular bursts of yellow-green. Someone was tuning in to a fuzzy-sounding top-forty station on a radio. Barely dressed teenagers chased each other; the girls shrieked when the boys caught them around the waist and whizzed them in circles fast enough to send their flip-flops tumbling.

Only one guy muttered "Go home, faggot," when T passed. He was dressed entirely in lemon yellow, from sweatpants to oversized T-shirt, even down to the sneakers and watchband, as if adding a second color to the ensemble would have confused him too much. The thin fuzz of a new moustache edged across his lip, like the gray-green mold that grows on old bread. He said, "Go home, faggot," under his breath, and nobody paid him any mind except one girl in a loose, Disney-themed T-shirt who rolled her eyes and said, "Shut up, David. You're ignorant." It was a good, clear night, but there was no sign of Twee.

Once home, T took ten dollars off the stack of bills Kohl had left for them all and went to the corner to buy three cans of SpaghettiO's and a pack of cigarettes. After smoking a cigarette while leaning out the window, T tidied up the piles of junk in the squat, restacked the coats on the milk crate couch, and tried to fix the little bullet hole in the wall that seemed continuously to vomit plaster crumbles. The best T could do was scrape away the debris and shove a milk crate in front of it so they didn't have to look at it all the time. The hole, unfixable without something that cost money (toothpaste or spackle or something), would have to remain.

Kohl and Peebo each returned from their days, sighing heavily and unburdening themselves of shoes and tight clothing barely seconds after shutting the door behind them. The three sat and waited for Vas. The stillness was thick around them.

Finally, Peebo said, "I'm starving," so they heated two cans of the pasta on a fire in the sink and ate straight from the tins without speaking. When they were finished, Kohl took the spoons and wiped them clean with newspaper. Peebo offered them saltines from a box he'd stolen from a market on his way home. They tried the whistling game, which didn't work on Kohl—she could whistle right through the salty dry crackers, no matter how many they ate, and for some reason that sent her laughing uncontrollably, spewing everyone with cracker crumbs and spit.

Even Peebo laughed and said, "Gross."

By the time the light was entirely gone, when they were moments away from closing themselves behind their blankets for the night, Vas showed up. He had a big slash across his cheek which had stopped bleeding some time ago, but which was still bright red and pretty dramatic.

"What the hell *happened* to you?" Peebo asked.

"You're bleeding!" T said.

"I fell," Vas said, which was clearly not the truth. The cut was too clean and even, and Vas was too adept to fall flat on his face like that.

"What'd you fall on, a knife?" T said.

Vas scowled. "I fell on a rock, if you must know. I was trying to climb over a guard wall because I saw something floating in the river and I wanted to get it."

"Uh huh, okay," Peebo said.

"Looks like you got slashed," Kohl said. "Not the work of a rock."

Vas looked at her and shrugged. "It looks like what it looks like. I fell, though. End of story."

"Let's hope it's the end of it," Kohl said.

"What's that supposed to mean?"

"Let's hope the rock didn't follow you home and isn't going to break in here tonight and all of us aren't going to *fall* on it in the middle of the night and be killed in a bloody horror show."

Vas had scrupulously emptied his face and voice of all expression, though beneath his skin the muscles twitched. He took one cigarette from the pack, tucked it behind his ear for later, and snorted. "You're welcome to sleep elsewhere," he said to Kohl. "I'm going to bed. *Here.* Where I *live.*"

He turned his back on them to crawl into his blanket-fort and violently whipped it closed. When Peebo stepped near, he shouted from inside it, "*Alone!*"

Peebo backed away, hands raised.

"Let's hope it's not a *gang* of rocks!" Kohl yelled at the blanket.

The fabric jiggled, as if Vas was moving around inside it too heartily, then went still.

"Spoiled ass," Kohl said. "He doesn't even think about what his selfishness does to the rest of us."

T couldn't say anything in Vas's defense. Vas had grown up rich—really rich. His family may have been immigrants, but they were the Sport Boat and White Polo Shirt kind of immigrants, not the Work Around the Clock Just for Food kind, like the rest of them had come from.

VAS'S DAD HAD BEEN SOME big merchant guy in Greece, and his mom had come from a long line of local politicians in Piraeus. They had moved to an overstuffed, yawning house in an unnaturally green suburb in central Ohio, where the neighbors cooed over Vas's father's "ethnic" good looks and "adorable" accent. (His mother—short and plump, with dark-olive skin and scant English—they left completely alone.) As a community-building effort, the Homeowners' Association had chosen a tree for each street in the development and required all its residents to plant that tree along the sidewalk in their front yards; cherry trees lined one street, Japanese maples or crabapples lined another. Boys turned tight circles on their skateboards on the blacktop driveways and girls practiced cheerleading routines in the front yards. Vas had been born in the hospital two miles away and grown up in that same house his entire life, the single child of a family that wanted and loved and prized him more than anything else in the world.

Even so, Apostoles Vasilakis was now more militant about the group's anti-materialist politics than any of the rest of them. Living with so little comfort was probably a lot easier when you had a choice in the matter.

It never really made sense to T—or any of them—why Vas had left his family in the first place. It's not as if they were awful people, or as if they'd kicked him out, or even as if he'd had to leave for the good of the family. He'd said, *proudly,* that he'd rejected all those comforts of home and *chosen* to live closer to the bone. He wanted to be *real,* not a spoiled, ignorant rich kid. It was an *important choice* he'd made; it was *political.* In fact, he often emphasized, he could probably go home any time he wanted, and his parents would welcome him back from the prodigal life. *That seemed to make the whole decision matter* less, T had always thought, *not more.*

"THAT IS TOTALLY A KNIFE slash, right?" Kohl said in a stage whisper.

Peebo looked at her, his eyes dramatically wide.

"We're *all* thinking it," she said.

"*I* was thinking it," T said.

"Duh," Peebo grunted, and shut himself into the bathroom.

"Is he going to *sleep* in there since Vas won't let him in the tent?" Kohl asked.

"No!" Peebo shouted from behind the door. A loud groaning noise let them know the pipes were creaking to life. A moment later, the shower kicked on.

"Two minutes!" Kohl yelled, because Vas didn't.

CHAPTER 6

ARRIVALS AND DEPARTURES

VAS DISAPPEARED EVERY EVENING AND reappeared a couple hours later. He wouldn't talk about what he was doing, but he always seemed a little quieter, a little kinder when he got back. Sometimes his eyes were red.

He'd get home and fold himself straight into his tent without talking to anyone. There would be no sound until he emerged in the morning in his red polo shirt, ready for work at the office supply store. Nobody asked him about it, since none of them wanted to poke the bear and ruin the kinder, gentler Vas. Peebo made a nest of coats on the milk crates and slept there. He didn't try to enter the makeshift tent, ever, didn't even complain about how stiff he felt in the mornings.

Finally, after two weeks had gone by, Vas came home after one of his evening disappearances, kicked his shoes off, dropped his bag by the door and announced, "I'm out."

"What?" T said.

"Of The Uproots. I'm out."

At that, Peebo sat up suddenly from where he'd been practically invisible, engulfed in the pile of puffy coats. He seemed to appear from nowhere, like some underfed, gangly-limbed genie with no useful powers.

"Wait, what?"

"I'm quitting the Uproots. I'm moving out, too, when I find a place," Vas said. "Nothing personal. I just have to get my life straight."

Kohl put aside the bowl she'd been wiping with a newspaper and handed Vas a dish filled with rice and some sad-looking lumps of potato, carrot and cabbage. "Here's your dinner. What are you talking about? You okay?"

"I'm fine," Vas said. "It's just personal."

That was the signal to stop talking, but nobody in the group was very good at picking up on signals, especially from someone as usually unsubtle as Vas.

"What happened?" T said.

Vas clenched his jaw, then sat next to Peebo on the crates and cradled the dish of food on his knees. "I've been going to N.A.," he said after a few hurried bites.

"N.A.? Like—"

"Narcotics. I'm straight now."

Peebo snorted, and Vas glared.

"I'll be gone as soon as I find a place."

"But wait, *what* narcotics? How could you afford drugs?"

"I got stuff from a friend at work. We always did it there. I never brought anything back to the squat and never spent any of our money, so don't worry."

"That is absolutely not what I was asking," Kohl said. "What narcotics? What kind?"

"Doesn't matter. We just want to know you're okay," T said.

"You just want to know my business," Vas said. "It's fine. I never did anything here. I just wanted to tell all you guys I'm sorry for being a jerk sometimes."

Peebo hadn't moved; jaw slack, he slumped against the wall amid the coats. He shook his head slightly. "Seriously," he said.

Vas glared at him again but said nothing. T felt the pressure to say something just to say *something* instead of the *nothing* Peebo seemed to be saying.

"It's fine," Kohl and T said nearly simultaneously. It was the thing to say, the automatic response you were supposed to give when someone says, "I'm sorry," but T, at least, didn't feel it. It wasn't fine at all. Vas had started the band *and* The Uproots; it had all been his idea, and he'd pulled the rest of them along with him and now he was going to leave them all dangling here with no stove and no heat and no nothing. Plus, he'd been a royal jerk lately, and they'd all put up with it and even taken care of him with dinner and cleaning, and he thought a flip "I'm sorry" was going to make it fine. (Not even an "I'm sorry," but an "I wanted to say I'm sorry," which really isn't the same thing at all.)

"Are you out of the band too?" Peebo asked.

"The band is already dead," Vas said.

"We can revive it."

"Then I'm out, yeah. I have to stop *everything* I was doing so I don't pick *any* of it back up." He looked significantly at Peebo, who snorted again and sank back farther until he was completely obscured by the coats.

It was clearly a mistake for Kohl to invite The Stupendous Kevin to the squat for dinner in the first place, but the timing was a worse mistake in light of Vas's announcement. Kevin arrived at the door that evening before they'd all cooled down and settled into Vas's news. There was a knock—a far too formal occurrence for a place in which they were illegally squatting—and there was Kevin: peppy, entirely shiny and polished; even his hair had been slicked back enough that it shone like Superman's. He glanced at the pile of shoes near the door, then at the gritty floor, then appeared to decide to keep his shoes on before thrusting a supermarket bouquet in Kohl's direction.

"Oh! This wasn't necessary!" Kohl said, stuffing her face into the purple mums.

"Miss Manners said a man should always bring a lady flowers."

"Miss Manners did not say that."

"Probably. I don't know," Kevin said, shrugging. "But a man should do it anyway."

Is grabbing a plastic-wrapped bunch of crappy supermarket mums really what Miss Manners would have had in mind? T kept quiet.

Kohl pressed her lips together in a tight smile. Then she seemed to think better of it and made the smile bigger. It almost looked genuine.

"Thanks," she said, pulling the plastic sheet off the bouquet.

"I climbed in the broken front window, like you said! Exciting! I felt like a burglar." Kevin beamed.

"Right," Vas said. "A burglar in a shiny red satin vest."

Kevin smiled again and smoothed the vest over his chest. "It's my show vest," he said.

Peebo stood behind Kevin, contorting his face into horrified poses and rolling his eyes so hard it looked as if he might hurt himself. "Hey, man," he said, suddenly composed, when Kevin turned around and stuck out his hand to shake.

"That's Peebo," Kohl said, breaking off the flower stems and stuffing the blooms into a used paper coffee cup with no water.

"Let me fill that in the shower," T said, then turned to Kevin. "Sink in here is for cooking. Doesn't actually run water, so don't try."

T grabbed the cup before Kevin could ask anything about the Cooking Sink or say anything more about what men should and shouldn't do or otherwise make the conversation any more uncomfortable.

"And that one scuttling away with the flowers is T," Kohl said as T hurried out of the room. From the kitchen area, T could hear Kohl correcting, "T, *T*, like the letter, just T."

To his credit, Kevin apparently let the matter drop after Kohl explained it to him because, when T returned, Kevin was all smiles and extended his hand with businesslike charm.

KOHL HAD SPRUNG FOR A head of broccoli and boiled it up with the standard onions, carrots and potatoes, then mixed in a healthy dose of curry powder, salt and stolen diner butter pats. She'd even made rice. It didn't taste very good, but it was different and fancier than they were used to, so it was good in that respect. Kevin appeared to be mildly disgusted by it, but he choked it down as best he could and tried to look enthusiastic.

"Is it okay?" Kohl kept asking everyone, as if overnight she'd been magically transformed from a serious graduate student into some sort of brown Donna Reed whose biggest concern was that her pot roast was moist enough—or her pot of abominable curried rice, anyway.

"It's great," Kevin said and smiled tightly. "Next time, I'll bring you some mushrooms and zucchini to toss in it." He made a big show of eating another bite very carefully so as not to glop onto the expanse of shiny red vest.

"Here, let me help," Kohl said. She grabbed a piece of newspaper and stuffed it into Kevin's collar, smoothing the sheet over the vest like a bib. "Got to protect that. It looks really nice."

"Thanks. It's my show vest," Kevin said for the second time, looking a little like a piece of fried cod stuffed into a newspaper cone. *All he needs,* T thought, *is the chips and malt vinegar.*

After dinner, Kevin crouched on the edge of a milk crate while Kohl wiped the dishes. Vas and Peebo leaned out the window to share a smoke. T took the clean dishes from Kohl and stacked them on the counter.

"Have you been doing this long?" Kevin asked.

"Doing what?"

"*This,* this homeless thing."

"We're not homeless," Peebo said from where he was bent over the windowsill. "This is our home."

"Right," Kevin said. "But not legally. And don't you all want real beds? Or a stove and refrigerator? A mailbox? Something easier, nicer, *cleaner*?" Kevin scraped his shoe against the gritty floor as if to prove his point.

"Those things come with a pretty high price," Kohl said.

"I bet you could afford it if you pooled your money," Kevin said. "I'll help."

"That's not what she means," T said and, when The Stupendous Kevin looked confused, T set down the dishes and said, "We're trying not to hurt anyone. Showers, electricity, gas stoves, all of it has impact. They eat up resources. And people die for those resources."

"Cars use up resources too," Kevin pointed out. "You have one of those."

"We only drive it when we need it to transport something. Otherwise we walk or ride the bus," Peebo said. You could see how much effort he was putting into liking Kevin, but it didn't appear to be working. Little beads of sweat had popped out along his forehead.

"Seems hypocritical," Kevin said, and that was the end of the night's gentility, such as it was. Even Kohl looked irritated.

"You're right," Vas said. "We should probably do nothing and be some turd of a kids' party magician or something."

Peebo snorted from the milk-crate couch on which he was reclining. "Dude," he said, chuckling. "Harsh."

"It's better than nothing," Kohl said.

Kevin brightened, as if he'd finally read the room. "You're absolutely right," he said. "We can't all be activists all the time." He pulled off the newspaper bib and began to fold it carefully, then thought better of it, twisting it into a long tail and waggling it in the air. "Trash?"

"Take it with you when you go. Use a can on the street," Kohl said.

"We *are* activists," Peebo said under his breath.

T FIGURED THAT WAS THE last they'd ever see of Kevin, but T turned out to be stupendously, stupendously wrong.

Most nights, they had no choice but to be in Kevin's Stupendous Presence and listen to his Stupendously Ignorant Lectures about The Uproots project (how cruel it was, and *have you ever been robbed?* and it was childish and selfish and—what's more—dangerous). They weren't even really doing Uproots work anymore, or they hadn't in a long time, but that didn't seem to matter to Kevin, who perched like Socrates at the center of the great room and pontificated for hours to any of them who appeared to be even half-listening. According to Kevin, it was better to do nothing at all (*like Kevin did,* thought T) than to break into people's houses and take their hard-earned stuff.

Kevin gave Kohl a Stupendous New Wardrobe. From time to time over the next few weeks, Kohl showed up carrying shopping bags full of Kevin's choices: three modest dresses, several sweaters and skirts, a couple pairs of shoes, and probably some lacy new underpinnings of which Kohl kept them all unaware. She left the shopping bags piled on top of her books in the middle of the floor like a message, the significance of which did not escape any of them.

Kohl seemed to realize how Stupendously Annoying Kevin could be and did her best to keep his mouth shut in their presence. She never argued, but skillfully redirected his thoughts when he started piously down a path they all knew would not end in a good place. T managed to keep quiet at these moments, but Vas could not stop muttering under his breath during every one of Kevin's sermons. Kohl noticed, even if Kevin was too full of his own voice to hear.

After his third visit, Kevin had left with a wave and a cheerful admonishment to all of them to *be good,* then leaned over to kiss Kohl on the cheek. He spent a dramatically long time whispering in her ear.

After he'd finally gone and they'd shut the door, all three of them, as if they'd planned it, turned on Kohl at once.

"Seriously?" Vas said.

"What?" Kohl said, a guilty edge to her voice.

"He is Stupendously Awful."

"You hate him?"

Everyone looked at Kohl, eyes wide in disbelief.

"It's not exactly that," T said. "It's—"

"It *is* exactly that," Peebo said. "We hate him. Dude sucks."

"Well, get used to him if you want to see me."

"What does that mean?" T asked.

THAT NIGHT, KOHL SHUT HERSELF behind her own long-abandoned blanket before T could ask what she was doing. She slept alone there every night that week. By the third night, T's skin itched and ached. Without Twee and Kohl, there had been no touch from anyone, not even a casual bumping-into on the street, in days.

Kohl was chipper and superficial when she did talk to T. She didn't stop by the laundromat anymore, didn't share secrets or opinions or inane chatter, and she threw herself hard into studying. Several times a week, she slept at Kevin's place. Most other days, she left early in the morning and didn't return until late at night, when she hurried quickly into the private space behind her blanket. She didn't help cook or clean, didn't share meals with them or take cigarettes from the communal carton. She wasn't present even when she was there.

T WAS SURE THE SQUAT kept a cosmic balance, because as Kohl faded away, Twee began to appear again.

The first time T saw her again was while walking home from the laundromat. Twee had set up her cage on the sidewalk near the front entrance of the downtown Eat'n Park and was in a heated debate with the restaurant's manager, a sloping woman in her forties. Her hair sloped sideways in its loose bun, her shoulders sloped downward, her body pitched forward at an angle. Everything about her was powdery and imprecise. The nametag on her green vest said BETH.

Beth wanted Twee to move the cage off the restaurant's property.

"It's not *your* property!" Twee yelled. "It belongs to the *public!* Out here belongs to everyone!" She was so thin that the brown smock dress she wore hung off her shoulders as flat as if it was still on its hanger.

"That may be, but the sidewalk here belongs to Eat'n Park. We keep it clean. We hose it down and pick up trash and sweep it. We shovel the snow in winter. We get ticketed if anything happens on it. And we don't want you scaring away the customers or causing trouble."

"I don't talk to anyone," Twee said. "I just sit in the cage. I'm not hurting anyone."

The manager looked at Twee, exasperated, as if she was torn between calling the cops and giving the girl some soup. "Take it somewhere else, okay, hon?" she finally said. She patted Twee on the shoulder and tried to smile kindly. "No offense, but a girl in a cage is bad for our business. If you're really not trying to hurt anybody, you should leave. You're hurting Eat'n Park."

"A restaurant is not a person," Twee said, but turned to fold up her cage.

T crept off before Twee could look up and notice she'd been spotted.

The next time T saw her, Twee did notice. She was crouched in her cage by the riverfront again, well away from any business that might complain. She had a new sign explaining, in simple terms, her project and promising cash to anyone who could get her to eat something.

"Hey, Afro Puffs, if you get me to eat that doughnut, I promise to give you a hundred dollars," she shouted at T.

T stopped walking, stomach clenching at the name again, and held up open hands, shaking them to show they were empty. "No doughnut!"

"I know," Twee said. "So you definitely can't make me eat it."

"No puffs, either," T said, patting the neat goddess braids that had taken Kohl all of the previous evening to achieve.

"I know. I just thought it was funny to say. Symmetrical, somehow."

"Twee," T said, squatting by the cage.

"I'm good," she answered without being asked. "Are you good? Is everybody good?"

"Nothing's good, it's all going to hell. But the gun is long gone. You should come home with me." T stuck a finger through the cage bars and waggled it in a *c'mere* gesture. Twee smiled.

"I'm at the shelter again. It's pretty okay. Clean," she said.

"Not safe, though."

"Safe enough, really. There's a good, hot shower, too, and you can stay in it forever if you want. Nobody yells. It's heaven."

"Come stay with us. Everybody misses you," T said.

At that, Twee furrowed her brows and frowned.

"Okay, well, *I* miss you, anyway," T relented. "Nobody else probably notices. They've all got their heads in other places."

"Right," Twee said. She fiddled a little with the handle on the cage door, then turned it to let the door swing open. She reached through the opening and pressed T's nose like a button. "Beep," she said.

T rocked back a bit, out of arm's reach, and said, "I'm serious."

"Okay," Twee said. She crawled out of the cage and unclasped the latches to fold it flat, propped it onto its luggage cart, then leaned the whole thing against her hip. "I'm not getting any attention here. I can pack it in for the night."

"I'll take it this time," T said, reaching for the cage.

"Thanks, but I got it," Twee said and hauled the thing forward.

WHEN TWEE RETURNED TO THE squat with T, nobody seemed to notice. She parked the cage in the lobby stairwell of the building, hidden behind a few crumbling cardboard boxes, and moved back into T's space without giving an explanation to or hearing a word of welcome from anyone.

That evening, it was as if she had never left: Kohl had splurged on a box of pasta, so she and T cooked it as best they could over the sink fire and served it with pats of butter and packets of salt and pepper Twee had stolen from the Eat'n Park before she'd been evicted from its sidewalk. They couldn't really get a hot enough fire going in the sink to boil the water, so the pasta was chewy, more as if it had been soaked in warm water instead of actually cooked.

"Nice," Peebo said, making a show of gnawing and crunching on the pasta. "Still beats the curry slime you guys have been making lately."

"You don't like it, then cook for yourself for a change," Kohl said.

"Right," Peebo said.

"Seems fair," Twee said, and suddenly Peebo looked at her as if he just realized she was there. "Thanks for making food, you guys," she said.

"But you're not eating," Kohl said.

"Doesn't mean I don't see what you do for everybody," Twee said.

Kohl actually smiled. "Okay," she said. "Fair enough."

Both T and Twee understood that she was really saying, "Okay, I'll share. You can have T too."

TWEE SLEPT IN T'S TENT that night, and it was as if overnight her chemistry changed and she unquestionably became one of them. In the morning, she moved with easy familiarity to heat some instant coffee she'd brought to share with everyone. That, of course, earned her an important place in their bricolage home. All of them thought so, even Kohl, who seemed to have put aside her irritation with Twee in favor of the coffee.

T thought it would be brilliant to get Twee a job at the laundry, which T did without considering that it might cut down on T's own hours and they would never be working at the same time so they'd rarely, if ever, see each other. Once a day, in the evening, they were together for only a few hours before collapsing into sleep. But Twee earned a little this way, enough to help with food and cigarettes, and she and T shared a wordless understanding of the washing machines' mechanical *chug-chunk-chug-chunk* that never left your ears, the sharp smell of bleach, and the detergent you could always taste on the back of your tongue, even first thing in the morning when you hadn't been near the laundromat for hours.

It was quickly getting colder; Pittsburgh was a city of extremes and seemed to go from unpleasantly sweltering and humid to unpleasantly cold and damp in a matter of weeks. Soon, the dank ground would ice over, and they'd be able to see their own breaths in the air, even as they bundled up and tried to fall asleep in the squat. They'd moved into the squat the previous year after the worst of the winter had passed, and so none of them knew what the place would be like in the real thick of the cold. Already it looked as though it would be bad. The windows actually shook when the wind blew too hard, and air whistled in through hundreds of little cracks.

Every night over dinner, they argued about whether or not to start Uproots work again. For Kohl, it was too risky; for Peebo, it was not risky enough.

"I just don't want to take chances like that anymore," Kohl said one night for what seemed like the hundredth time. "We could get in real trouble, breaking and entering. We're technically stealing, even."

"We're technically Santa Claus-ing them also, since we always leave something as an exchange," Peebo pointed out.

"Something we stole from someone else," Kohl said.

"In the end, it all works out to be even," Vas said. "Besides, who cares? *Eat the rich.*"

Twee and T sat silently on the milk crates. T kept a hand curled around Twee's knee, squeezing every once in a while to remind her to keep quiet. She have any business weighing in on this, and when Kohl and Vas got going at each other, it was like a runaway train. Best to stay out of the way. Instead, they followed the volleys as if they were watching a ping-pong match.

"I care," Kohl shouted, thumping the kitchen counter so hard she made the plates rattle. "Have you ever thought about what it might be like for someone to come home and discover we've broken into their home?"

"That's exactly the point," Vas said. "Thanks for joining us!"

"But not everybody is going to feel it the same," Kohl said.

"From each according to his ability, to each according to his need," Peebo muttered. He was lying on the floor with his feet propped up on one of the milk crates. He barely moved when he spoke, so the effect was like a ghostly voice rising up from the building itself.

"What?" Vas snapped.

"Peebo gets it, at least," Kohl said. "What if we break into the house of a woman living alone? Or someone who's been robbed before? Or someone who's been attacked, or worse?"

Vas shrugged and rolled his eyes. "What if one of your so-called victims wears fur? Or drives a huge car every day? Or buys clothing that some ten-year-old in the third world died making?"

"Politics has to be local, too, you know!" Kohl screamed. "You should care about the ten-year-olds *here*. Some of the people we're terrorizing probably have kids, and how do you think those kids feel? It's not just the third world that's struggling. What happens in Pittsburgh is just as important!"

Nothing important happens in Pittsburgh, T thought.

Vas opened his mouth to yell something back, but Peebo suddenly stood up and held out his hands. "Shush! Shush! What is that?"

"What is what?" Vas said, but both he and Kohl stopped screaming and listened.

From behind T and Twee came a faint and muffled rhythmic whirring smack. Peebo dug under the coats until he found it.

"Oh," said Twee when she saw the monkey figurine that Peebo had uncovered. It had begun to go on its own, head jerking forward and back, plastic cymbals clapping.

"That is chilling." Twee leaned closer into T's side and shivered.

"You brought it here," Kohl said. "Chickens coming home to roost, now?"

"I thought we lost that thing a while ago," Peebo said, sticking a finger between the cymbals to stop the plastic clumping sound.

"I thought so, too," Vas said. "Spoooooky!" he yodeled, wiggling his fingers in the air. Twee dug deeper into T's side, as though Vas's fingers were actually threatening.

"Like herpes," Kohl said smugly.

T shuddered and stood up suddenly. "Taking a shower."

"Two minutes or less," Vas said.

"That's four rounds of 'Twinkle Twinkle.' Singing it out loud is super therapeutic," Twee added helpfully.

T disappeared into the bathroom, and they all heard the pipes groan and shudder. Peebo turned the monkey over to see if he could find a switch or something to stop the monkey from clapping. It was starting to creep everyone out.

A moment later, T came out of the bathroom, dry, still clothed.

"Hey, everybody," T said, and everyone looked over. T paused, then delivered the news: "Water's shut off."

CHAPTER 7

LOSING

KOHL STOLE A PACKAGE OF baby wipes from the Giant Eagle (*they can afford it and we can't,* she told the group imperiously), but they had to buy a couple jugs of water for drinking and cooking since those were too big to swipe easily. The cheapest they found was about seventy-five cents a jug, which was doable, but it was that distilled water probably not meant for drinking.

When they got back to the squat, T swigged from the jug and passed it to Vas, who swigged and passed it to Kohl as if they were teenagers sharing a clandestine bottle of schnapps at a football game. Kohl eyed the jug and took a swig, then frowned.

"This is distilled," she said, reading the label.

"It's what we could afford—it was on sale," T said, "and it's what we happened to pick up. We don't have cash for another jug right now. It's still water." T walked the jug over to Peebo, who'd declined to join them at the counter but was making hurry-up-and-gimme gestures at them from his place on the milk-crates. T stood and waited while Peebo chugged, then took the jug back to the counter and handed it to Vas.

"Beggars can't be choosers," Vas said and took a gulp. "Water should be free, though. It's a human right."

"But we're not beggars," Peebo said. "We *are* choosers. We chose *this* situation because we have morals and standards. That's kind of the whole point."

"Whole point of what?" Vas said, whipping around to look at Peebo. Vas was pressed against the counter, trying to cut a stolen apple into pieces with a plastic knife. He stopped to glare. Peebo sighed.

"I guess I don't even know, man."

"Our teeth are all gonna fall out—it doesn't have the minerals or stuff in regular water," Kohl worried.

"You know this from your science degree? I'm pretty sure you're wrong about that. It has something to do with the polarity of the atoms or something, that's all," Peebo said. He sat like a smug Buddha, cross-legged amid the coats on the improvised milk-crate couch he seemed to have claimed as his place.

"You ass, you don't even know how they distill water. That's not how it works. They take the minerals out. That's why people put it in irons."

"I don't think either of you should ever be a chemist," Vas said. "Water is water. You don't get your vitamins and minerals from water. It's just wet. That's why we have the apple." He sawed at the fruit until the plastic knife snapped in half. He tossed a couple apple slices at Kohl. "Vitamins. Freshness. Original sin."

"Right, like we need more sin." Kohl took the apple anyway.

At that, Vas showed them the gaps in his gums, a couple molars already gone. "The wages of sin, ladies and gentlemen...and T," Vas said.

"Seriously? What is your problem? Phobic much?" Kohl snapped.

Twee pulled T to sit with her just inside the shelter of the tent, probably to diffuse the sharp feeling of the conversation. T sat stiffly. Twee put her arms around T's neck and kissed, but T shrugged her off.

Outside the tent, Kohl said, "Do you have to be shitty every time you want to make a point?"

Vas shrugged and continued to grin widely, then chomped his teeth a few times for effect.

"When did *that* happen?" T said, waving a hand at the gaps.

"Probably swallowed them in my sleep," Vas said. "Or maybe they eloped. There's two gone, so who knows." He grinned like a jack-o'-lantern and took another swig from the water jug.

"Did you lose them at the same time?"

"Like I already said, *who knows*? I didn't keep track."

Kohl looked revolted. Vas leered again, consciously stretching his lips back to expose the gaps when he did; he seemed to enjoy being the source of her horror. The missing teeth should have sat right on top of each other, so the effect of their absence was a doubled gap. He pushed the tip of his tongue out through the space.

"So we're losing body parts over this now," Peebo interrupted.

"It's what the life costs," Vas said. "Not like I need them to chew through fresh vegetables or meat or anything."

"Actual pieces of ourselves, gone," Kohl said.

"*My*self, not yours," Vas said. "You've got Fancy Magic Man now."

"That's not fair. I'm here, aren't I?"

"Right. In that really swanky outfit." Peebo scoffed, sinking deeper into the pile of coats in which he lay. This time, T gently embraced Twee and pulled her closer into the shelter of the tent, as if they could hide from the blowup that was clearly brewing in front of them. Twee didn't resist.

"It was a gift," Kohl said testily, smoothing the skirt over her legs, then unceremoniously reaching up under her skirt with a baby wipe as if nobody were watching. She scrubbed at her thighs, then behind her knees and down her shins, then rubbed at the bottom of each foot.

"Not a thread loose in the entire ensemble. So shiny," Vas said.

"If the number of holes on your person is a measure of your worth, then Twee and I are one up on you, darling," Kohl said, tossing the spent wipe onto the counter.

"Was that a crack about me not having a vagina?" Vas said.

"Take it how you want to take it," Kohl said. "It's *your* lack."

Twee looked terribly uncomfortable to have been pulled into the argument and put, without consultation, onto a team. "I think…" she started to say, but Vas and Kohl kept arguing as if she weren't even there.

T squeezed her shoulders and grinned, whispering, "It's just how they do. Let it go."

"I think you've got that backwards," Vas snorted at Kohl. "Freud said it. It's *your* lack, isn't it?"

Kohl laughed. "Freud? You're listening to Freud now? I guess repressed homosexuals flock together."

"Low blow," T muttered, and Kohl narrowed her eyes.

Twee had wriggled out from between T's arms and sunk entirely into the tent. She sat cross-legged on the bedding, picking at a scab on her ankle. She didn't even seem to be listening anymore, but T knew better. The weather, as if it had decided upon irony, was golden; the setting sun's rays pressed in through the windows and inched across the floor like lava slowly coming for all of them.

"You're arguing about private parts? What about T?" Peebo said.

"My body's not up for discussion," T said. "That's why people call them 'private parts.'"

"I don't," Twee put in uselessly, apparently addressing the comment to her ankle.

"I just mean if we're going to get priggish about body parts and gender and who's better, you mess up Kohl's argument."

"I'm not involved in this," T said. "It's a ridiculous argument to be having, and it doesn't matter anyway. You *act* like a dick, you *are* a dick, whether you have one or not." T felt Twee snicker. Kohl looked down at the counter, turning and turning the jug of water between her hands. She didn't look as if she was paying any mind to the conversation anymore, but she wore a smug grin.

Peebo put up his hands. "The end. You're both waylaying the argument anyway. This is about missing *teeth,* not whether or not someone has a *you know what.*"

"Mature," T said.

"Peebo's right, though," Kohl said. "It's not okay. Vas's teeth fell straight out of his head."

"Or into it," T put in.

When Vas shot T a look, T smiled. "I'm pretty sure he swallowed them. He likes to swallow, right, Peebo?"

They all looked a little stricken—it was pretty mean, especially coming from T, who was usually so unshakable and even. Kohl's mouth hung open, and she made no attempt to close it.

Vas reached up onto the top of the fridge and grabbed the pack of cigarettes. There weren't many left, but he shook one out anyway. He opened the fridge, took one of Peebo's sweaters, and squeezed it over his head. Everybody watched him, waiting for a reaction, as he tugged his coat out from under Peebo on the crates, threw it over his shoulders, and opened the door. He stopped, turning to aim a glare at T. "Hypocrite. Especially coming from you."

"*Especially* me? Why do I have to hold myself to a higher standard than he does or you do?" T looked long at Vas, going for implacable but probably coming across as more tired than anything else.

Peebo didn't say much after that, not for two whole days, and then he left the squat for good. That morning, he oozed off his milk-crate-and-coat bed, shoved an armful of clothes into a plastic bag, pulled on his ripped-up sneakers and Vas's too-small pink puffer jacket and stood at the door.

"Okay. So. I'm going," Peebo said over his shoulder.

"Okay," T said. "Can you pick up cigarettes while you're out?"

"No. I'm *going* going. Like, out of here. Like, done with this whole mess. Like, for good."

"That's my coat," Vas said. He hadn't moved from where he was sitting on the floor near his blanket-tent, but he was staring at Peebo with a pinched mouth and narrowed eyes, like a dare.

"Yeah, I don't really have a coat anymore, and it's freezing out. I'll give it back to you tomorrow. You're not going anywhere today anyway."

The jacket looked ridiculous on Peebo. He was a good deal longer and taller than Vas, and the sleeves only covered his arms to just past the elbow and left his spindly forearms poking out, painfully vulnerable and bare. The bottom of the jacket didn't stretch to his waist, either, and stopped short just a couple hands' length below his armpits. It looked like a fluffy, hot pink bolero jacket.

"What? You're moving out? Vas hasn't even found a place yet," Kohl said.

"I've got a place and I need a shower," Peebo said. "Baby wipes make me smell like a diaper."

"You smelled like a diaper before that," T said, but Peebo didn't acknowledge the joke.

"How did you find a place?" Vas asked. "I still can't find a thing."

Peebo looked uncomfortable. Vas waited, staring, until Peebo gave up.

"I got some money," Peebo said. "I'm renting a place in Homewood."

"Seriously?" Vas said.

"Plus, if you got money, why go *there*?" Kohl asked.

"It's not a bad neighborhood," Peebo said. "It just has a bad reputation."

"They'll eat you alive," Kohl said, shaking her head. "Homewood's tough."

Peebo snorted. "I'm tough, too, little girl."

"Right. Okay," Kohl said, laughing a little. Then she narrowed her eyes. "Where'd you get the money, anyway? Talking to Mommy and Daddy again now that you need them?"

Peebo didn't say anything. He went to the fridge and took the last of the cigarettes from the top of it. He started to shove the whole pack into his pocket, but T yelled, "No way!" so Peebo shook six out, put them in the plastic bag, and put the rest of the pack back on top of the fridge.

"Mommy and Daddy," Kohl confirmed with a sneer. "Spoiled and selfish."

"Whoa," T said.

"Whatever," Peebo said back. "I got money from a friend. A *real* friend. A rich guy who wants to help, too. My parents don't have money. But you wouldn't know, would you? You think everybody has what you had."

"I—" Kohl said, then stopped.

"What about The Uproots?" Vas asked after they'd all been quiet for a long, uncomfortable minute.

"We haven't been doing The Uproots."

"We were going to start again," Vas said.

Peebo looked as if he was about to laugh. "Really? We *were?*"

When Vas didn't respond, Peebo nodded and said, "Yeah, I thought so. You're completely full of chickenshit. Principles are great until they cost *you* something, right?"

Peebo shook his head, so Vas said, "Rent boy."

Everybody held their breath. Peebo pulled the ludicrous jacket as closed as he could get it over his chest, picked up the plastic bag of his stuff, and left.

"Well," Kohl said. "That's that."

She jiggled the pot of water over the fire she'd made in the sink, trying to force the instant coffee crystals to dissolve faster. Their coffee was often chunky and lukewarm because they couldn't really get a big enough fire going in the sink. Vas was scooping peanut butter straight from a jar, not bothering with bread. He made one last scoop, then screwed the lid back on and shoved it across the counter at Kohl.

After a long silence, Vas said, "He has a point."

"What point? He's taking money from some sugar daddy like a—"

"Plus he stole half our cigarettes."

"Well, at least he's not going to be a hypocrite. Or stink anymore." Vas licked his fingers, then shut himself into his janky blanket-tent. He emerged minutes later wearing two sweaters and a knit hat, then left the squat. He didn't come back until long after Kohl had left for Kevin's place and T and Twee had gone to bed.

THE BABY WIPE BATHS GOT old after two days: They clouded up a sickly smell of baby powder and rot, and they didn't do much to help with getting clean, much less washing hair. T felt lucky to have put in the braids before all the mess happened so that it wasn't as much of an issue, but Twee and Kohl were miserable.

When T came home to find Kohl shaving off the sides of Twee's hair, it started to look serious. There was already a clump of Kohl's hair on the counter, and both sides of her head were glowing and freshly bald. A long strip of black hair ran down the middle of her head to her back, and she kept tossing it back and forth like a mane as she worked on Twee.

"What happened to your deliberate asymmetry?" T asked.

Kohl shrugged. "No shower. Felt gross on my neck. Time to get even."

"We're getting ahead of the problem," Twee told T, and ran a finger across Kohl's newly naked scalp. "Get it? A *head*?" Kohl flinched away but kept working with the razor.

"Okay," T said.

"Want to go next?"

"I'm good." T patted the fat braids Kohl had put in. "What will Kevin say? That's not very Princess Jasmine of you."

"Kevin doesn't get a say in how I wear my hair," Kohl said. "It's my body."

"He'll probably make her get a wig, but it's worth it, right?" Twee added, nudging Kohl.

Kohl looked right through Twee and sighed. She scraped the razor up the side of Twee's scalp, and the hair fell into a pile of little yellow needles on the floor. T bent to scoop them onto a piece of newspaper. "Like I said," Kohl repeated, "it's my body."

"It's also your job to be Princess Jasmine and look amazed at his flying carpet trick and then let him saw you in half," T said from the floor. Kohl laughed a not-laugh, which was enough of an answer.

"So you guys are friends now?" T asked, standing up.

Twee held still while Kohl kept shaving the side of her head, but she strained her eyes sideways to look at her.

"We're sisters," Twee said.

"We're not sisters," Kohl said.

"No, I mean like a metaphor, like sisters in the cause," Twee said, making a salute with her fist.

Kohl looked at her blankly. "We're not sisters in anything. But we're good. We're on the same side, at least. And I won't murder you in your sleep."

She tapped the safety razor against the now-bald side of Twee's head, and Twee gave a half-hearted laugh.

VAS DIDN'T COME BACK FOR two days, and T wasn't sure whether or not to worry. When he reappeared, he was scrubbed and shaved, and he smelled like coconut oil. Kohl, Twee and T had been leaning against the counter, eating dinner together, but when Vas burst in, they froze.

"What happened to you?" Kohl said. She was the first of them to move, putting down the forkful of glop she'd been hefting toward her mouth. Twee put her fork down, too, just because Kohl did. She'd quickly become Kohl's shadow, walking close behind her, doing everything Kohl did, and trying to adopt her easy air of confidence. Kohl, for her part, seemed to like having a duckling, and even occasionally dropped her irritation in favor of a small kindness: a nod of agreement here and there, and even an occasional quiet smile at Twee's paltry jokes.

"I, my friends, have discovered the joys of unlimited hot running water, and there is no going back!" Vas stuck out his chest. It made the pink jacket, which he'd somehow recovered, look even smaller.

Kohl scowled. "What about your principles? If everybody can't have it, nobody should?"

"Okay," Vas said. He knelt by his blanket-tent, dismantling. "But I smelled like a zoo in the summer. I work at a place where they will fire me if I smell like I did. I need the money."

"Principles," T said. "Where did you find a shower, anyway?"

Vas didn't answer right away; he busied himself making a sloppy pile of the blanket and his few T-shirts. He grabbed his pillow and began to unstuff it, tossing crumpled newspaper and bits of yellowed foam on the ground at his feet.

"You cleaning that up?" T asked.

Vas didn't even look up. When he finished unstuffing, he set to stuffing the blanket and his T-shirts into the pillowcase.

"Principles," T said again, head shaking.

"So where *did* you find a shower?" Kohl asked.

"Peebo's new Homewood mansion, for sure," Twee said.

Vas stopped stuffing and looked at Twee long and hard. The girl had a distinct lack of guile, which made her seem like a juicy little sheep blinking back at a wolf. Twee looked nervous, then scooted toward the bathroom and closed the door. It was the only door in the squat, aside from the front door, though it was one of those cheap hollow plywood deals, and everything that happened in the bathroom could be heard from anywhere else in the place. They could all hear Twee talking behind the door, probably into the mirror. It sounded like she was saying, "You're okay, you're okay, you're okay.

"At Peebo's." Vas went back to cramming his stuff into the pillowcase.

"I think you broke Twee, you jerk," T said, rushing to the bathroom door and rapping lightly.

"You *going* going, or do your principles still matter at all?" Kohl said. It wasn't even a question, really.

Vas hefted the pillowcase onto his shoulder like a jeans-and-sneakers-wearing, olive-skinned Santa Claus. *An especially skinny and beardless and perpetually ticked-off one,* T thought. T rapped on the bathroom door again, but Twee had gone silent and wasn't answering.

"I'll be back," Vas said. "I'm just going to spend a few days at the new place."

"Right, okay," T said.

That was the last they saw of Vas for a long time.

WITHOUT PEEBO AND VAS, LUCKMONKEY was just two poorly played guitars and no singer, so the band fell apart pretty quickly and officially, with no promise of reuniting.

In actual fact, it wasn't so much a falling apart as a gentle dissipation, a wandering off. Plonking away on an ampless guitar seemed to T a little like trying to walk uphill wearing lead shoes, and Kohl had sold her guitar and couldn't sing to save anyone's life. They only had to argue once over who would have to sing "Awful Stroller Baby" or any of their other terrible songs that Vas had always somehow sung believably before they realized how ridiculous Luckmonkey had become, as foppish and useless as Wham! or Pepsi and Shirlie, and then it was most definitely over. Neither of them suggested practicing or spoke about trying to find a gig; and neither ever mentioned the band again.

Even so, T held onto hope and couldn't sell the guitar just yet, even if it would have given them more money for smokes and food. The guitar and the horrible cymbal-playing toy were all that was left of Luckmonkey now.

They put the windup monkey on the gold-flecked counter in the center of the kitchen, where it stared at them, its cymbals pulled wide apart, its head back, looking like a held breath or an unsaid thing. It seemed more like a threat than a reminder, and while nobody wanted to think about it, nobody could bring themselves to get rid of it for good.

Every once in a while, one of them would swear they saw it whir and clap a couple claps, then go still again. But it was always out of the corner of an eye, and it didn't happen for more than a moment, so nobody was ever really sure. Twee tried to convince them the thing was haunted, though haunted by *what* she couldn't really explain.

"You've watched too much *Twilight Zone* or something. We're not throwing it out. It's an important reminder of our past mistakes," T said from inside the blanket-tent. Kohl was in her own tent for once, and Twee was floating around somewhere in the squat, clanging things and making bumping sounds. T had no idea what she was doing.

"You mean *my* mistake," Twee said. There were a couple emphatic bumps.

"Okay, it's a reminder of our *principles,* then." T lay on the bedding inside the tent and stared up at the top of the blanket, which had been cinched and tied with string to a bulbless hanging lamp. The fixture swayed a little as Twee stomped back and forth and bumped things around, and the tent swayed with it like a giant undulating sac.

"Exchange one for one, take nothing." Disembodied and irritated, Kohl's voice floated out of her tent. "That'll teach us."

"*I* took it, not *us,* so you mean that'll teach *me,*" Twee said. She crawled into the tent with T and sat down, sighing. Her face was red and sweaty, despite the chilliness. "I should be the one to get rid of it."

"Go on, then," Kohl said like a dare. "Get it out of our lives already." She hurled the monkey into T's tent, where it bounced and rolled to a stop at Twee's foot.

Twee stared at the awful thing. Its grin was a mocking grimace, with an open mouth of huge teeth and bright red lips. Bloodshot, too-wide eyes, matted brown fur, red- and white-striped pants. No shoes, but its tan-bottomed feet had little articulated toes. Twee shivered.

"I don't want to touch it."

"So there it will stay until you *do,*" Kohl said, nodding smugly.

"Let that be a lesson to you, young lady!" T warbled like a schoolmarm.

"It's not a joke. That thing is a constant reminder," Kohl said. "It's the ugly, undead manifestation of our hypocrisy."

"Feel the wrath of the Evil Monkey! Look upon its furry undead delight!" T said and Twee laughed. Still, T kicked the thing farther away from the bedding, just to be on the safe side.

Kohl's irritated silence was heavy. "Seriously," she said after a moment.

"It's the lesson that just won't die," Twee said. "The Truth that Ate Pittsburgh."

"Night of the Living Monkey," T said.

"The monkey that keeps on giving," Twee said.

"Ghoul Interrupting. Little Drummer Beast."

"Okay, enough," they heard Kohl shout. "Plus, those are *cymbals,* not drums."

"Primate Evil," T said.

They heard a scuffling outside the tent, then the slide of the cigarette carton on top of the fridge, then Kohl saying, "Back later," and the slam of the front door.

TWEE SUGGESTED THEY TRY STARTING The Uproots work again, especially since the band was dead. They needed something. It seemed weird without Vas or Peebo, but T and Kohl decided to give it a go anyway.

They didn't have too many choices of where to go without Peebo's truck, and Twee insisted that they should, from now on, only hit businesses, since stealing from someone's home was so personal, and they had no way of knowing if they were hurting someone who had less than they did or maybe even scaring someone who was vulnerable. So they chose a place within walking distance, a shabby little computer repair place called House of Ill Compute.

"We should break the window just for that bad pun of a name," Kohl said.

Turned out they didn't have to break a window, because someone had left the alley door cracked like an invitation. T kneed it all the way open.

"We'd better be quick, in case they're coming back," Kohl said, slipping in. "We don't want another kid walking in on us or something." She said it, but they all knew it was highly unlikely, since it was nighttime and everything else around them was closed.

The three of them shuffled into the back end of the little shop. The plastic carcasses of sick and deceased computers were piled everywhere, innards junked in metal heaps, circuits and wires and pliers and scissors.

One tube of Crazy Glue. One pair of plastic safety goggles. A curling poster of a Charlie Chaplin rip-off sitting in an all-white room, hands poised above the white keyboard of a white computer, mouth a surprised O, as if he'd been caught surfing the Internet for sparkling white, silent-movie porn.

Twee held the wrapped fertility statue tenderly, like a baby.

The protrusion had been castrated when, in a rush to get out and get going, Twee slammed the squat door on it. The needle tip had broken off and fallen—they could hear it rolling around on the floor behind the squat's closed door but hadn't seen the sense in stopping to retrieve it. The mission came first. They would have to deal with the castrated appendage when they returned and found it lying, bodiless, on the floor.

"Forget it," T had said. "It's fine, let's go."

Twee had looked unsure and hesitated.

"It's dong-less now," Kohl had said. "That will be very disappointing to someone."

"We've all got to live with what we've got or not," Twee had resolved, and hopped down the stairs. T had sighed. Twee tried, maybe, at least.

Now, in the computer junkyard's dim windowlight, Twee looked around for a proper place to put the amended statue, then gave up, pushed some junk aside from the top of the workbench, and gently placed the statue there. It looked weird among the metal and wires and piled-up crap.

"It will provide some much-needed, updated décor in here," Twee said proudly.

"Yup, nothing says classy like a stretched-out figurine of a guy with a dangerously sharp broken penis," Kohl said. "But what do we take in exchange?" Kohl looked around. She poked a computer shell. "This stuff is either worth way too much or it's worthless crap. I can't tell."

"I'm going with crap," T said.

"We definitely shouldn't take any tools," Twee said. "Or we'll shut down their whole business, and that isn't fair."

Nobody argued, so they bumped around the workshop, searching. Nothing looked as though it could be taken. There was no sense of urgency about the hunt—T was pretty sure there was no silent alarm—so they did a pretty thorough job and made sure to keep the mess exactly as it was. Who knew what tech genius owned the place and what kind of organizational madness he might employ, madness they were too dim to understand or even notice? T realized they were probably giving somebody too much credit. Even the high-tech computer stuff looked ancient and worthless.

"This," T finally said, giving up and thumping the back of a padded vinyl desk chair. "It's got wheels, and they have two more. Losing it will be a minor inconvenience at worst and it won't screw the business."

Kohl nodded and held open the alleyway door. T wheeled the chair out into the night. Twee lingered, scanning the workbench as if trying to put things back in order. *So much junk!* she mouthed. When she realized they'd gone and nobody was paying her any attention, she scrambled to catch up.

"Can I get a ride?" she chirped and threw herself into the chair T was pushing. "Home, James!"

"It's not a game," Kohl snapped. "Get out of that!"

Twee got up. "Sorry," she mumbled. "Just trying to lighten it up a bit."

"It's not *supposed* to be light! You're *supposed* to be thinking about what you're doing to someone else's life and what that means. Otherwise it doesn't mean anything and it's just a selfish prank."

"We've got to go three blocks," T said to Twee more kindly. "There are cracks and bumps on the sidewalk. You're going to end up on your ass is all."

"Got it," Twee said. She managed a wavering smile and walked on ahead.

T gave Kohl a look, one with raised eyebrows and buggy eyes, one meant to ask an irritated question like *what the hell?* Kohl bugged her eyes right back and held up her hands emphatically, as if to say, *I should ask you the same thing,* then looked away and walked ahead. T pushed the chair in a shaky rumble over the sidewalk. By the time they got to the squat, the plastic wheels were worn and pitted, and T's hands were numb.

"WE FORGOT TO LEAVE A note!" Kohl said suddenly, just as they were all drifting to sleep. They'd dispensed with tents in favor of using the blankets as bedding and closeness for warmth, so the three of them lay curled up in a single nest made from all the bedding pooled together, with half the blankets under them to create a soft, warm layer between them and the cement they could feel under the thin wood parquet. T lay between Kohl and Twee, silently wishing for more space, but grateful not to have had to choose which of them to sleep with. Kohl had thrown her arm protectively across T's chest and her leg across T's knees, as if grabbing as much real estate as she could. Twee curled, her back to T, in as tiny a ball as she could manage.

"What? We forgot what?" Twee said, sleepily urgent. She sat up suddenly, as if the squat was on fire.

"A note! We forgot to leave a note at the computer place to explain what we did! Now they'll just think they were robbed, or some kids broke in there or something."

"They might not even notice anything at all," Twee said, rubbing her jaw.

"That is *not* a better scenario," Kohl said.

"Shit," T said. "Should we go back?"

Kohl held T in place, refusing to move, and looking as if she was thinking it over carefully. T had no choice but to wait. Finally, Kohl patted T's belly and shook her head. "It's too late. And it's too risky. We just need to be more careful and more thoughtful next time." She looked directly at Twee. "It's not a game, and we can't be playing around."

Twee nodded. "I get it," she whispered. She looked teary again. "Next time."

T wasn't sure there should be a next time. Without a truck, they were pretty limited in where they could go and what they could take. Still, the situation of the world hadn't changed, just their own resources. That couldn't be much of an excuse for doing nothing.

CHAPTER 8

CAUGHT

Dear homeowner:

Congratulations! Your possession has been Uprooted.

Do not be alarmed: you have not been robbed, nothing has been damaged and no one has been harmed; your ___coffee maker___ has simply been repossessed by the universe. Since it was made of atoms that move freely and belong to no one, it was never yours to begin with, but only appeared temporarily to be in your home. It could have stood anywhere, had the atoms collected in another place instead of here. Do not mourn its loss, for it is not gone; rather, it has been absorbed into the Great Exchange.

To compensate for the loss you probably feel, the universe has left you this ___very nice desk chair___ . Please enjoy!

—The Uproots

WHEN THEY'D BROKEN INTO THE office park, it was because Twee insisted that they were still hitting the Little Guy and they should be aiming at Business. The computer place had been a little too little for everyone's comfort.

They'd let themselves into the main building of the complex—Twee had actually let them in, thanks to a rock and a skinny arm. She'd cracked the glass of the front door enough that she could reach in and unlock it, and, from there, it was easy to get into the lobby and the main hall. Problem was, after that, they would *still* have to break into one of the offices.

"Let's hit the dentist, in memory of Vas," Kohl said, jiggling the door's handle.

"He's not dead, he just left."

"Okay, in memory of Vas's teeth, then," Kohl said.

"That makes no sense. Besides, what would we take? Who's going to want a dental drill?" T asked.

"Definitely not me." Twee went sprinting down the hallway, jiggling door handles and peering into the occasional plate glass window.

"This is a bust." T wheeled the office chair to the side of the hallway and left it there, out of place and useless, like those sneakers people hang on telephone wires.

"Here's a ladies' room," Kohl said.

"Don't they lock those things? Don't you have to have some sort of official key to get in?" T asked.

Kohl tried the door—it pushed open without resistance.

"It's our lucky night," she said. "The ladies' is open!"

"That just sounds bad," T said. "Anyway, what are we going to take, tampons?"

"*And* pads. We'd be liberating them for the good of femalekind if we did. They charge an arm and a leg for something that should be free," Kohl said, skipping backward into the bathroom. "We could distribute them to homeless women."

It actually wasn't a bad idea...maybe better than what they had been doing. T filed it mentally under Things to Consider, and then, without a second thought, followed Kohl into the mirrored lounge.

The ladies' room smelled like powder and lavender, probably some sort of freshener spray that made it seem cloyingly less fresh. It was close and windowless: cinderblock walls glopped with insistently pink paint, disintegrating posters (Picasso's "Fleurs et Mains" and a shrunk-down version of a Monet water lilies painting in a fake gold frame, and, for some probably horrifying reason, an anti-choking poster). Every wall was hung with mirrors. There was a basket of silk flowers and, next to it, a couple crumpled paper towels in a soggy mess on the sink counter. Kohl was already pawing into a pack of spare toilet paper, oblivious to anything else.

"Toilet paper!" she whispered. "We can redistribute this to homeless people on the street, or to shelters or something! Should I take the whole box? No, no…we have to carry it. I'll just get some, though."

T's stomach twisted at the sight of both of them in the mirror. While Kohl rummaged, not even glancing up, Mirror T stood frozen, like a mouse caught on the counter when the kitchen light goes on. T stared at the unfamiliar image of the person in the nubbly brown turtleneck sweater and low-riding jeans. Fat goddess braids stretched down the image's head; a soft halo of escaped hair curled out; grim mouth, lips pressed into a tight line; softly widened eyes; a little galaxy of deep brown freckles on the cheeks. Alien.

It was rare to catch an actual mirror (usually the closest T got was a reflection in the dry cleaner's window on the way to work, since the mirror in the squat's bathroom had been stolen long before they moved in), but coming face-to-face with such a clear and exact image in *this* space tipped the floor sideways so hard T almost slid off into nowhere. The picture burned, permanent and unreal: the glittery, off-limits territory of the ladies' room with T at its center, simply standing there.

With the squat now waterless, they all used the bathroom at the gas station a block over—it only had room for one person at a time, so it wasn't too bad as long as the nasty clerk wasn't working, since he usually chased them off before they could pee. T usually avoided big public bathrooms entirely, because no matter which one T tried to use, it was bound to look like the wrong one to somebody. That could mean serious trouble. It was easier to hold it, even for hours. It was like that old gameshow where you had to choose a door to get a prize. T could win trouble behind Door #1 or trouble behind Door #2.

Damned if you doo-doo, T thought, and snickered. At least there was a private staff washroom at the laundromat.

The only substantial thing in the ladies' room that wasn't screwed to the wall was a smelly, flowered settee in the little mirrored antechamber. Kohl lifted the end of it, just to test the weight.

"This?" Kohl said.

"It smells horrible. Like someone swallowed baby powder and then threw it up."

"I guess we couldn't even get it anywhere anyway." Kohl sat on one of its graying cushions. "We'd have to carry it home and then carry it to the next place. Unless we just kept it. A couch would be nice."

"The smell, though," T said. "Can you imagine smelling this all the time?"

"I'm probably going to absorb the smell too." Kohl jumped up. "It's like a horror movie. *The Smell* or something."

"That would be our punishment for being amoral and selfish," T said, trying to eye Kohl significantly. "For keeping it instead of putting it into the Exchange."

Twee burst in. "You guys!"

"Jeez!" Kohl said, holding her hand to her heart. "Don't ever do that again!"

"Sorry," Twee said, lowering her voice. "But you guys! I got one!"

"You got one what?" T asked. Twee danced back and forth in the doorway, and it made T nervous. The girl never seemed to stand squarely on two feet; she was always in motion, like a chipper little shark, and T wondered what horrible ways her body might malfunction if she stood stock-still.

"There's a kitchenette in the hallway down there." Twee gestured emphatically, as if they could look through the wall. She was so excited she was almost out of breath. "If we took something, it would be from the whole building, not just from one little place!"

"All right," T said.

"It's fairer that way! Come on!" Twee burst back out of the ladies' room. They heard her go running down the berber-lined hallway like a kid playing tag.

"Fairer?" Kohl mouthed silently, and T shrugged.

"How does she have so much energy if she doesn't eat?" Kohl asked, holding the bathroom door open.

"Feel lucky that she doesn't eat, then. Can you imagine?" They left the bathroom and looked for Twee in the hall.

"Come on, you guys!" they heard her whisper-shout, and she peeped out from behind a corner at the end of the hall and beckoned wildly. T and Kohl jogged to meet her, and, as soon as they rounded the corner, Twee spread her arms like a gameshow model.

"Ta-daaaa!" she sang quietly. "Check it out!"

It was a kitchenette—just maroon countertop interrupted by a stainless-steel sink and a couple oak cabinets, really—but on the counter were a coffee maker, a basket of plastic-wrapped muffins, and some mugs.

"You want a coffee break now?"

"No, silly, we can take something. A mug or something!" Twee held up a chipped white mug with a cartoon of a fat orange cat wrapped around the front.

"A *mug*? Do you even get what we're trying to do?" Kohl turned to leave.

"The coffee maker?" T said.

Twee looked ecstatic. "We could use a coffee maker!"

"It's not for us. We take it but we don't keep it. It goes into the Exchange and gets passed on to the next place," Kohl said. She unplugged the machine and lifted it off the counter. It was hulking and metal, almost as big as Kohl was. Her arms looked stringy in comparison.

"Dump the pot and the filter or we'll have a horrible mess," T said.

Kohl balanced the machine on the edge of the counter, and T took the pot with its puddle of leftover cloudy coffee to dump in the sink.

Kohl pulled out the filter basket. In it was a dried-out, molding filter of used coffee.

"This is gross. These people do not deserve coffee," Kohl said. T laughed and rinsed the pot. Kohl said, "Do you really think they'll even miss the coffee maker if the filter had time to *mold*?"

"It's Pittsburgh." T swished the pot under the faucet to get at the stray bits of whatever gross thing had been growing and floating in it. "Everything molds in three minutes if you let it sit still."

Kohl replaced the filter basket, hefted the machine onto her hip again, and wrapped the cord around her wrist so it didn't dangle. Twee stuffed several packets of coffee and a couple plastic-wrapped muffins into her pockets, and the three of them hustled down the hallway and back toward the front door.

Before they reached the end of the hall, they could see that something was very wrong.

Outside the broken front door, lights whirled blue and red and blue again, and a cop was bending over the hole Twee had punched in the glass.

"Oh shit, oh shit, oh shit," Twee muttered, clawing at T's arm.

"Shut up," Kohl hissed. She barely seemed to hesitate before she dropped the coffee maker on the carpet and bolted back down the hall. "Come on!" she called over her shoulder as she went. Twee turned and ran after Kohl. "T! Move it!" Kohl hissed. Twee and Kohl took a sharp turn around a hall corner and disappeared.

The coffee maker was on its side; the pot rolled in wet circles on the carpet. T set the pot straight—*why bother?* T thought, but did it anyway—and was about to run when the cop, who'd managed to rattle the front door open, looked up and yelled, "Stop!" T froze.

"What are you doing in here?" the cop said. His uniform—polyester, navy—pulled snug across his chest and around his thighs. A black leather belt strung with unnecessarily well-equipped utility pockets was cinched around his hips. The radio there toggled between silence and a fizz of shouted directions and background noise. T stepped backward toward the empty lilac hallway down which Twee and Kohl had run, debating whether to run for it or stop and give up.

"What are you doing in here?" the cop said again. "You speak English?"

"Yes," T said. "We—"

"Turn around, face the wall," the cop said, and T obeyed.

T SAT IN THE BACK of the police car with arms twisted uncomfortably behind so the metal cuffs ground into T's back. Lights whirled, and everything outside the windows went *go-stop-go-stop-go* in a blur. The plastic seat provided no traction, and the seatbelt was loose, so T couldn't get a solid purchase on the seat and slid back and forth in minute but uncomfortable shifts until the car finally pulled into the station lot. The two men in the front seat got out. One opened the back door and unhooked T's seatbelt, saying, "Come on." T got out, overbalanced, and the concrete swung up. The man caught T and held on until everything was put right again, but the parking lot was still swinging wildly, lit up and strange.

"He's gonna faint," the cop said. "Help me. Get his other arm."

"Whoa, fella," the other cop said, grabbing an arm. "Steady. Go slow."

The men flanked T, lifting up and forward as they walked. T was strung between the cops, feet dangle-walking until they were inside the yellow-green, too-bright fluorescence of a station house. The men guided T through the open frame of a metal detector. One of them ran his hands like creeping spiders up and down T's legs and under T's arms.

"We're good, all clear," he said to the other guy, and they dropped T onto a bench, and then T waited for what felt like hours but was probably only moments.

T's shoulders ached from the backward pull of the cuffs. Leaning forward was the only position that stopped the ache, but that way the world heaved unpredictably and T's balance kept slipping. Leaning back helped the balance, but then nausea and soreness crept—*on little cat feet,* T thought bitterly—up T's spine and the back of the neck, across the face like a mask, until everything was a clouded blur. The station was so quiet and still; the only sounds were of shuffling papers and throats clearing, feet scuffing the linoleum, the occasional chair scrape. T's eyes were dry and itchy, and T tried to rub them with a shoulder, but it wasn't enough to clear up the burning blur. Finally, a man came to sit next to T on the bench. He had a clipboard and a Styrofoam cup of milky coffee.

"Mr…" he said and waited. His finger traced the bite marks he'd left in the top of the cup, then tapped it a few times. T looked at him blankly. Then the man said, "I need to fill out these forms, okay? And I need you to tell me the information. You don't have any ID. I need your name."

The man was short and soft and white, with his hair nearly shaved off. The skin of his scalp shone through a thin fuzz and made him look old, though he could have been thirty as easily as fifty. His eyes were rimmed with red, as if he hadn't slept in days.

"T," T said. The man looked at T and raised his eyebrows.

"T what?"

"Just T."

"T-E-E? Or T-I?"

"Just the letter."

"Okay," the guy said, furrowing his eyebrows. "Just the letter. You need to give me your real last name, though."

"Persaud."

"T Persaud. What is that?"

"It's my name."

"Where's it from? Persaud… it sounds British."

T sighed and looked at the man. "I live in Pittsburgh," T said.

"Okay, Mr. Persaud, all right. Just curious." The guy sighed, sipped the coffee, and looked at T with a tired expression. He leaned back on the creaking bench, stretched his back against the wall, then righted himself, cleared his throat, and moved on. "Your address?"

T hadn't really thought about it before.

"Address?" the man repeated.

"Not really," T said.

The whole conversation was useless—T couldn't give the man much of the information he asked for, and the man didn't ask T any of the correct questions. The form was completely wrong. Sex? The man had circled *M* without even asking. Race? He'd written *Black*. Address? *Homeless*. Medical Conditions? He'd left that blank, but underneath it he'd written Intoxicated.

What an incredible power, T thought, for the cop to get to decide all those answers.

"I'm not drunk," T said.

"What's that, Mr. Persaud?" The police officer was kind. He had raised his voice an octave, as most men do when they talk to their mothers. He wasn't at all what T expected at a police station.

"I'm not intoxicated."

"Okay," the man said, but left the form as it was.

THE POLICE OFFICER LEFT, CAME back moments later cradling a fresh cup of coffee and explained that the questions, the fingerprints, the humiliating pat down during which there had been, against protocol, a very curious audience, all of it had meant that T had just been booked and would stay in the station house's holding tank until arraignment. First, however, they were going to ask T some questions to get the full story of what had happened at the office park. Given the hour, arraignment wouldn't be anytime soon, so there was no rush. The policeman asked if T wanted to call someone, but there was nobody T could think of to call.

Another man came to the bench. He was sloppy and puffed-out, and his polyester uniform had absorbed the too-strong smell of sweat and cologne.

"Come on, Boy George, we're going to talk," he said.

"T," T told him as the first man handed the second man the clipboard.

"Mr. Persaud," the new guy said, as if *he* were the one who should correct *T* on the matter. He pulled at T's elbow until T got up and tripped after him down the hall and into another office. He pressed T into a wooden chair with sticky, scraped-up varnish, and then slumped into another one.

"Mr. Persaud," he said, looking at the clipboard. "Let's get this all straight."

HE WANTED TO KNOW WHY T was in the office park and he wanted to know what T had been planning to do before the cops showed up, but none of T's answers seemed satisfactory. Despite T's insistence to the contrary, the cop was pretty sure T had been trying to break into one of the smaller offices inside the complex to steal cash or drugs—the dentist's office probably had plenty of those.

When T said with a frustrated sniff that there were much better places to find drugs if one wanted to do that, the cop scoffed. "You were looking for Novocaine," he said, like a statement. He tapped his pen on the table once: period.

"No," T said, "I wasn't. I was giving them a chair."

"What?" The cop's face reddened, the creases staying white, until he looked as stark as a woodcut. T shifted and pulled at the handcuffs, ready to duck if necessary. The cop had the look of an angry father.

"A chair," T said carefully. "I left it in the hallway."

"You broke into a place *not* to rob it but to *give* them a chair," the cop said, as if it was the dumbest thing he had heard in all his years on the job. It probably was. "What are they going to want with a chair? Why would you do that?"

"It's a project," T said. "It has to do with private property."

"Okay, sure, fine, you were leaving the chair, but you were also looking for the drugs."

"What would I do with Novocaine?"

"Sex stuff, right?" The cop leaned forward with narrowed eyes, grinning Cheshire and mean. "You on the stroll?"

"What stroll?" T asked. "What sex stuff?" It made absolutely no sense.

"Don't get wise," the guy said. "Like weird, kinky, S & M sex stuff. Whatever freaky-deaky gay thing you like to do." His rubbery face had gotten pinker; the creases between the pinched rolls had gotten whiter. He leaned forward into T's space, and his eyebrows were raised so high they had almost disappeared.

"I don't—"

"You get paid?"

"No," T said emphatically. "I don't even know what—"

The cop sighed heavily, leaned back, and scribbled in spiky, slanted handwriting on more forms, shaking his head as he did. At the end, he told T to sign one of the forms below where he'd written his own explanation of T's crime, including that T had been "seeking drugs" and was currently "inebriated" and "belligerent." The air seemed to be swarming and swirling, and the guy was sighing impatiently. The irritation came off him in waves like heat.

"We can get out of here once you finish this," he kept saying, so T just signed with a shaky pen. The cop took the pen, then pulled at T's elbow. They went down the hall and out the back, and then there was another bench and more waiting, then a little room containing two dirt-crusted old men, a stainless steel toilet and a stainless steel sink. They took off the cuffs and left T there to wait out the night with the men grumbling and fucked-up and eyeing T sideways.

T didn't sleep all night—instead, T watched the other two men who, by some mercy, kept to themselves, snoring and farting and cursing as they slept. The dark-haired one lay flopped and spilling off one of the wall's fold-down metal pallets, the one closest to the toilet. He seemed to be guarding it, though T dreaded using the toilet in front of onlookers and wouldn't have tried it anyway, no matter how desperate things got. T had become an expert at holding it.

The other man lay on the floor against the opposite wall for no reason T could figure, since there were plenty of bunks available. The dirty floor must have been worse than the cold metal slab, but maybe the guy knew that the senselessness of the choice made him seem all the scarier.

In the morning, someone took each man away in turn and, finally left alone, T tried to sleep and ignore the ringing and slamming and voices, the over-bright light, the awful smell of old urine and bleach and the grinding pain of a too-full bladder T couldn't chance relieving in such an unprotected place.

T woke to more clangs and shouts. The whole place echoed like a school gym. T's bladder throbbed, and so T crept to the toilet and squatted, trying to urinate and hide at the same time, getting urine everywhere. At least the holding tank was still empty.

T spent the long day staring at the banged-up, gray-green door and its little window of reinforced glass. The door opened three times, and three times an irritated man was led in, pulled down one of the metal bunks, crawled onto it and turned on his side to face the wall with a heavy sigh. Every time a loud metal creak. Every time a glance at T, a snort, a question: *What are* you *looking at, faggot?*

T kept awake, muscles tight, but stayed curled on the metal bunk and looked at nothing but the gray-green door. There was no clock, no natural light by which to tell time. T stared at the door until a rhythm developed: the sound of feet shuffling past, a clang, voices, more shuffling, quiet. Occasionally they came in and got one of the guys in the room with T. This happened again and again, until there were three of them left.

One of the guys, tall, stringy, with a pot belly that paunched over the waistband of his pants, paced in circles, mumbling in Russian or Polish or something similar, occasionally stopping at the door to shout in the direction of the station room on the other side.

"Shut up," said the guy who'd taken the bunk by the toilet. "Shut the ever-loving Christ-on-crutches *up*!"

The Russian-or-Polish guy didn't stop or slow his pacing; something seemed wrong with him. His hair was several inches long, but pieces of it stuck out in spikes that he never stopped, not for a second, twirling with his finger. Occasionally he'd switch hands in a seamless operation: the second hand would find a hank of hair and begin twirling one second before the first hand would drop.

"If you don't sit down," the first guy growled at him, "I'm going to kill you. Don't try me, you fat Russian shit."

The crazy guy ignored him, or didn't understand, but T, for one, didn't doubt for a second, and prayed the cops would come back and take somebody out before one snapped and the other one got killed. T didn't care which one they took and which one they left behind— the unpredictable crazy twirler or the violent furious guy, it was all equally awful.

Finally, toward midafternoon, they took T out of the cell, leaving Twirler and Furious behind. They put T in a van with three other zoned-out passengers from the other holding cell. When T slid onto the only empty seat, the one on the bench farthest to the back, the man there shouted and covered his nose. "Officer, man, this dude pissed himself!"

The guy who had climbed into the driver's seat ignored the shouting and snapped his seatbelt closed.

"Officer, man, this guy smells like piss! I can't sit here!"

The driver silently shook his head and turned the key in the ignition. The guy next to T kept shouting about the smell, threatening to sue the police department, threatening to throw T out of the van, threatening all sorts of unrealistic but intricately described hell to pay. T tried to curl down and inward like a pill bug, until there was nothing exposed but the curved shell of T's back, until the guy's shouting had faded to an angry muffle and the driver banged the van over the speed bumps and out of the lot.

Streetlights and stoplights and buildings crawled by the van's windows, and then another parking lot, another building, more clangs and buzzers and doors slamming and men talking. Then all of the first cops were gone and someone else took T down more hallways and into a small room with folding chairs and a nicked-up plastic table. A woman wearing a thin gray suit came in, flopped a huge leather purse down next to one of the chairs, and introduced herself as T's public defender. She was businesslike and sharp-boned and so quick she seemed almost unkind. She was done and gone so fast T barely knew what they'd discussed.

T waited in the folding chair until someone else came in, and then they went down another hallway and into a wide room where the public defender waited, and they put T next to her. A judge said they wanted money to let T go home to wait for a trial, even though T's public defender argued that would be disproportionately punitive for someone like T. The other lawyer said that was exactly the point, that T was transient and would probably disappear into the streets, and the judge agreed, and then it was done, and that's when T's knees gave out completely, and T couldn't stand to follow the officer down the catacomb of hallways to the van.

Somehow, T made it to the van. Somehow it was empty except for T, and the ride to the jail was uneventful. Somehow, *somehow*, Kohl was already there when the van brought T to the jail, and after what seemed like an endless amount of waiting and form-filling and more waiting, they let Kohl pay money and take T home.

"I'm so sorry!" Kohl said as they left the building. Her eyes were wet and red. "I tried to get you before, but they wouldn't let me until after the court thing. They sent me home yesterday." She wrapped her arms around T's neck and sobbed. T felt like a stone, stiff and cold; it hurt to stay bent, but Kohl wouldn't let go. Finally, T pulled away and stood upright.

"It's fine," T said. "It's fine. It's not your fault."

"But we ran. We never should have left you behind. I didn't realize you weren't with us until it was too late."

"If you'd stayed, we'd all have been arrested, and nobody would be there to bail us out. It's fine," T said.

They had to walk to the bus, but Kohl had bus fare for both of them, and the weather, for once, wasn't terrible, so the walk was almost pleasant, and their bus came uncharacteristically promptly. They sat on the wide bank of seats at the back, away from the smattering of riders who'd collected toward the front. The bus climbed up and down hills and pulled around corners. Kohl and T slid back and forth on the plastic seat, clinging to each other for what little stability they could manage. It wasn't too long before they'd made it back to their stop and walked the several blocks to the squat.

The moment they opened the door, T hurried for the bathroom. The door closed onto privacy, the floor was mopped clean, and the room smelled like the dank air shaft into which the bathroom's window opened. T nearly cried from relief and, right after peeing, took a double dose of Premarin. T had no idea if that was dangerous or if it would do anything to compensate for the missed day's dose, but didn't want to take the chance.

When T opened the bathroom door, Twee was waiting. She rushed up tearfully and threw her arms around T's neck.

"It was the worst night! I didn't sleep at all!" she cried.

"Were you listening to me in there?" T asked, but Twee didn't even seem to hear the question, weeping quietly into T's chest as she was. T pecked Twee's cheek and pulled away, then headed for the counter at which they ate their meals.

Kohl handed over a bowl full of some sort of brown-flavored stew she'd cooked, and Twee brought a jug of musty-tasting water. T swigged straight from the container, then offered it to Kohl, who shook her head.

"Thanks," T said, and dug into the food. "I haven't eaten since yesterday morning. It's good." It wasn't good, and it had gone cold, but it was in a bowl from home and someone had made it just for T.

"I made you a fluffed-up bed," Twee said. "After the jail bed, I bet you want something nice." She'd literally piled all their clothes under a blanket on the floor. It looked as if she'd stolen or somehow bought a few cushions and stuffed those in there too. "I might have even made it *too* soft."

"Thanks," T said, feeling waterlogged. A ringing in T's ears wouldn't stop.

"I doubt it's *too* soft," Kohl said, but there was no fire in it. She looked haggard; her eyes were drooping closed. "I imagine you just want to go to bed after all that. I know I do."

"It's not even six," Twee said. "Stay up a bit."

"How did you bail me out? I owe you forever," T said, still shoveling in food. T felt bottomless.

"You don't owe me a thing," Kohl said. She was twisting and untwisting the edge of her shirt around her fist. "I couldn't think about anything else until I got you bailed out. It was selfish."

"How?"

"How was it selfish?"

"How'd you get bail?" T asked.

"The Stupendous Kevin!" Twee burst in. She was already wiping the cooking pot clean with newspaper and dancing from foot to foot to some music in her head.

Kohl nodded. "Kevin stepped up."

"That really is actually stupendous," T said.

"He's a pretty good guy when you give him a chance."

"I see why you like him, despite the Show Vest."

"He has his moments," Kohl said. She stood behind the kitchen counter, wiping the same spot over and over with her bare hand as though she was trying to soothe the counter. T narrowed a suspicious eye, but didn't have the heart to call her on it at that moment; Kohl looked, however, inappropriately misty.

"Just don't jump bail!" Twee pinched T's cheek. "You don't want to leave Kevin holding the bag. Even *he* can't make that disappear."

Kohl rolled her eyes, and Twee did a *ta-dahh* kind of bow with her arms spread. "Get it?" she said and winked. Suddenly, T saw her in a new light. Maybe she wasn't quite so dippy and innocent. Maybe she was in on the joke after all.

"My appearance isn't until almost summer," T said. "But I'm not going anywhere."

"Good," Kohl said. "Don't go anywhere ever." She came around the counter and hugged T from behind, fitting her chin over T's shoulder and smooching T's cheek. She brushed her hand over T's braids, tucking a few stray hairs back in and licking her thumb to smooth the rest down. T tried hard not to flinch. "You're a real mess," Kohl said quietly and sniffled.

Before it had even begun to get dark outside, the three of them curled together on the lumpy makeshift bed and were asleep so quickly none of them even noticed drifting off. All night they lay pressed together; not one of them rolled away for more space or air, and their arms wrapped tightly around each other so that the three of them formed a snug, unsolvable knot.

CHAPTER 9

THINGS END AND THEN THEY BEGIN

EVERY DAY WHEN T WOKE up, there was a brief moment when things were quiet, and everything seemed stable for once. Right after that, consciousness would rush back, and T would remember the looming court date, and then the awful grinding feeling would slam in like a wrecking ball.

The three of them decided that they couldn't risk any more Uproots work with T's trial impending—nobody wanted to give a judge any more ammunition against T than they already had. With both the band and The Uproots done and gone, T felt purposeless. All that remained was a long and fairly ineffectual life of counting out quarters for dollars and cleaning out lint traps, a life of orange ice-cream-scooper chairs and the Sisyphean monotony of the laundry spinning around and around and around in the driers. Everything was ending, all the good parts of what they did had gone skittering out of their grasps, and the only sure things left were the crappy squat, the hard floor, the missing things, the hunger, the boredom, and the pointlessness of sticking with it.

ON MONDAY, KOHL DIDN'T GO to her evening class; she opted instead to lie quietly, thigh to thigh, with T on the makeshift bed. They talked about childhood memories—Kohl didn't even seem to notice that T contributed nothing, but only listened to her talk on and on about her older brother Jadu, who had married at eighteen, and her grandmother, who'd told her she didn't look in the mirror enough, who'd told her not to go walking around at night because men would leap out of the bushes to rape her, who'd told her, finally, not to come crawling back to the family when she left to go to school in Pittsburgh and inevitably found out it was too hard. Her mother and father had stood silently behind her grandmother, her father stiffly distant, her mother red-eyed and tight-mouthed, but neither had said a word.

Her grandmother had been kindly indulgent of young Kohl—she had been called Kajali then—and her rat's nest hair and skinned knees. She had, however, become firmly disapproving once Kohl had reached sixteen.

"Kajali, mere pria, always rushing, but to where?" she'd said. Her hand wrapped around Kohl's wrist like a too-tight gold bangle, cold and inflexible.

Kohl tried to twist her arm out of the grip but was stuck. "My room. I have a pile of homework."

"Homework, psh!" her grandmother waved her free hand. "Where does this get you? You will need glasses soon, from all the reading."

"That's not how it works, Grandmother," Kohl said, trying to keep the irritated edge out of her voice.

"I know what I know. You will learn," her grandmother said. She pulled Kohl's arm a little closer to her round, hard belly. Kohl could feel her breathe in and out. "Your mata and pita try so hard, and it is not easy for them with you. It is good that you study, but you must be a better daughter."

Kohl rolled her eyes.

"I know what I know," her grandmother repeated. "When you were a child, it was Oh-Kay," she pronounced carefully. "But now it is time to grow up and act like a young woman. You cannot be a wild child always."

"I'm sixteen, Grandmother, not a child. And I am not wild. I am trying to study to go to college."

"College!" her grandmother snorted. "How will you be a mother like this? Always what you want, never thinking of your family! Always *me, me, me, me!*"

"Grandmother, Mata and Pita want me to go! Just because you didn't—"

Her grandmother slapped her. Her usually soft eyes had gone cold and black, and all warmth had drained from her face. "Mere pria," she said quietly. "How dare you speak to your paradadi like so? You are a rotting fruit, going bad so quickly. If you go on in this way, not one single man will have you. You will have no home. You cannot stay with us here in our home."

"What?" Kohl felt bruised. She had never heard her grandmother's voice so flat. Her grandmother released her grip on Kohl's arm and turned her back.

"Kajali, you have responsibility to Mata and Pita and me. Nobody wants a daughter like this, who does not grow up into a woman, who does not bring children or a husband of her own, who stays like a selfish child only doing what she wants at every moment. Who only brings shame and costs us money, money, money? Nobody ever wants a daughter like this."

So school had been hard-won for Kohl, and it meant everything. She'd pushed through her undergraduate degree in three years and went straight into grad school without taking a breath or a walkabout or a drinking vacation like most of the kids she knew. Skipping her Monday class, in light of all that, was unlike her. But then Kohl skipped her Tuesday afternoon class, too, and it became bigger than just a much-needed day off. Cutting Tuesday was strange, because on Tuesdays was the post-colonial lit class Kohl really loved, taught by a young, exciting professor she also adored. She'd talked about the class so much that it seemed as familiar as if T had attended it in person.

"Why'd you skip Po-Co today? You sick?"

Kohl had joined T at the laundry. The two of them were sitting behind the desk counting quarters into efficient, ready-to-go stacks in preparation for a rush that didn't really happen on Mondays.

"Just didn't prepare, so I figured I shouldn't go," Kohl said. "Besides, it's just Said today, and I've read Said out the ying-yang. I'm not missing anything."

"That's not like you. You're like a Girl Scout with that stuff, always prepared, always duty-bound and dependable." T moved the stacks of quarters back and forth just for something to do, stacking and restacking. "And always with the cookies."

On the laundromat floor, some kid was pitching a fit, wailing at his mother. She tried to soothe him and get him to drink from a little bottle of juice while simultaneously trying to fold her laundry on one of the peeling pressboard tables, read a fanned-out novel, and shove a handful of peanuts into her mouth. *Probably the only meal she's had all day,* T thought. She looked like a harried octopus.

Kohl shrugged. "Must've lost my compass or something. Tossed my cookies. Some Girl Scout-related pun."

T squinted at Kohl, refusing to be distracted by her terrible attempts at jokes. "Lost your compass?"

"I don't know. Not an outdoor girl, really. I do the macramé."

"You're trying to lure me down a rabbit hole of bad Girl Scout-themed metaphors," T said.

"They happen to be fantastic Girl Scout-themed metaphors."

T had nothing to say. Kohl was being deliberately obtuse, and there was no chance of getting a real story out of her when she started down the path of rhetorical distraction. Instead, T studiously counted quarters into stacks and pretended it was the most important job ever.

Out of nowhere, Kohl began to kick T's ankle and make little whinnying sounds. When T shot her a look, she sat up straight and clapped a little and bugged her eyes at the laundromat door, where the Proper Old Lady stood with a small bag of laundry. She wore, as she always did, a delicate-looking pair of white gloves and a tilted, peacock blue church hat with an oversized blue silk carnation stuck to the front. Her massive purse dangled from the crook of her elbow.

"The P.O.L.; it's the P.O.L.!" Kohl looked ready to burst.

Despite being wise to Kohl's tactics of misdirection, T couldn't help feeling a little happier and chiming in. The P.O.L. was, for both of them, a bright spot of mystery in the dingy parade of undistinguished and predictable clothes-washers. She appeared irregularly, and as if out of nowhere when they least expected to see her. Their game was to invent a history for her—and the more fantastical, the better. Kohl was convinced she was a ghost.

"Okay, so she was a telephone switchboard operator and she met the love of her life over the phone. She connected him to PENNSYLVANIA-6-4208, which—"

"I'm serious," T said, continuing to stack quarters. It was nearly painful not to look up to spy on the P.O.L., but T knew doing so would only help Kohl redirect attention.

"So am I," Kohl said. "Almost always."

"Okay, then, so what's the real story? Why no PoCo today?"

"Dropped it," Kohl said.

"I will not drop it," T said. "It's important. I'm worried."

"No, *I* dropped *it*. Like, I dropped the class." Kohl had pulled her feet underneath her on the chair's seat, curling herself as tight and dense as a cannonball and resting her chin on her knees. She looked as if she was trying to get as small as possible.

"You what?"

"*Now* you can drop it."

"No, absolutely not. You love that class. You come home every Tuesday and tell me about The Fabulous Professor Nat Hino. You love her. You love her class. You love the books. You even love the people in the class."

"Yeah, well," Kohl sighed. She paused to hand a stack of quarters to the kid waving the dollar at her, then turned back to T. T put feet flat on the dirty cement floor and leaned forward. "Don't freak out at me, though," Kohl said. "I'll have to get up and leave if you do, I swear." She took a dramatically deep breath, squared her shoulders, and said, "I dropped out of Pitt."

T felt backed into a corner, because of *course* T wanted to freak out. What's more, T had not really agreed, not even with a nod, *not* to freak out, but still felt bound by Kohl's demand to stay calm. The washing machines went *a-chug a-chug a-chug*, and the TV yammered, and T couldn't think right.

In as measured a voice as could be managed, T said, "You dropped out of Pitt entirely? Like, out of the entire graduate program? Why would you do that? You love that place. Every time I see you, you're reading a book or you want to talk about a book or you're at least carrying a book with you just in case you get a chance to read or talk about it."

"I know," Kohl said. "It might just be for now. I need time to think and to get myself together. I can always go back if I miss it."

"You *can't* always go back," T said.

"Okay, well, I get almost a decade before they turn me away, so it's close to always."

"That's not what I mean," T said. "I mean you'll think you can go back, but then stuff will get in the way, and then you'll get a job that is more important, and then you'll get married and get a Crock Pot and a vacuum cleaner and move away and have babies and you won't want to think about stuff anymore and it will be too late."

"Since when does that whole routine sound anything like me?" Kohl scowled and thumped her feet up onto the desk, spilling stacks of quarters. She barely noticed. T slid off the chair and knelt to grab the coins that went rolling under the desk before they could get too far, but quickly got up again—it was absolutely disgusting under the desk. There would have to be gloves or a towel involved in getting those quarters back.

"You know exactly what I mean," T said, taking the seat again.

"I need money and for once I'm going to take care of myself first. I'm exhausted from all this." Kohl gestured around the filthy, packed office where they sat: the carboard box full of little packets of detergent, the cash box stocked with quarters, the tipped-over pen container, the paper cups of weak coffee, the cruddy floor. On the other side of the counter, a few laundry-doers sat like zombies cupped in their chairs, watching the TV even though it was always the same canned laughter and the same commercials for the same stuff they'd never be able to afford, the same awful sameness again and again.

"I got a job," Kohl admitted.

"Wait, what?"

"Being Jasmine. For Kevin."

"I already knew that. I've seen the outfit," T said. "It sparkles. Hard to forget."

"I mean he asked me to do it permanently. It'll be more money. It's not ideal, but it's going to pay some bills, and I need to get myself to a point where I don't have to think so hard about whether I can afford a small cup of shitty coffee from the convenience store. I can't do anything like this anymore," she said.

"Do what like what?" T knew exactly *what like what* Kohl was talking about but wanted to make her say it out loud. Kohl's declaration felt as sudden and cruel as pushing T out of a moving car, as if Kohl were without warning backing out of a long-established plan. In fact, T realized, it was almost exactly like that.

"I can't break into places and take stuff anymore. Worry about what's happening to you when they take you to jail. Cook tasteless glop over a fire in the sink. Rub baby powder in my hair so I don't stink because I can't shower. Keep my sweater and hat on at night because I'm freezing. Sleep on the floor and wake up sore every day. I can list more things if you need me to."

"No, I get it," T said. "But just because you don't want to do *this* doesn't mean you have to do *that*, you know."

Kohl snorted. "Right. I'm young. I have so many options," she said. "It's the dilemma of every bright young brown girl: just far too many opportunities in life." She sounded angry, but she looked sad, as if she was near tears again.

"Don't get obnoxious with me, that's not what I meant. I just mean you're too smart for being Princess Jasmine."

"Really. You think what I do with Kevin is stupid." Kohl had her finger raised, pointing it at T. She poked T in the shoulder a couple times for good measure. T stiffened at the painful touch.

"Yes, really. I think what you do for Kevin is sexist and kind of racist and absolutely stupid and beneath you, yes. You're way too smart for all that."

"Beneath me. Really? You've never even seen me do it," Kohl said.

The TV was playing a soap commercial; shiny, well-groomed people posed in the shower and tried to look extra clean, tossing sparkling white towels over their shoulders and smiling with straight, white teeth. The people in the laundromat didn't look even remotely that clean. Most of them wore their Laundry Day Clothes—torn, stained, unfashionable, too small—and had probably neglected any kind of ablutions before shuffling out of their apartments with their baskets of filthy laundry. Everything there—the dryers, the TVs, the people, even the air—looked yellowed with age and about to fall apart.

"I've heard you talk about it enough that I don't need to see you do Princess Jasmine to know it's racist and stupid. And," T added and grimaced, "I've seen that ridiculous outfit you have to wear, with all the beads and sparkles and fake jewels. The one that barely covers your boobs. You hate it. And it makes you look like you just escaped from a magic lamp."

Kohl was quiet. She held her coffee cup against her mouth, as if she was trying to block anything from coming out of her. Her eyes teared up and looked glassy. She didn't make a noise but she did shake her head *no* when T asked if she had anything to say.

"Look," T sighed. "I just don't want to see you give up on what you've wanted ever since I met you. You're smart enough to do anything you put your head to. You don't have to run around dressed like Barbara Eden and be some exotic and femme-y sideshow and wave your arms to demonstrate how great some guy is while he saws you in half and gets paid to do it."

"That's not fair," Kohl whispered.

"No," T said. "No, it's not."

WHEN TWEE GOT FIRED, IT seemed like the last straw on an already-shaky camel's back.

Twee always worked the later shift at the laundry—the place stayed open from six a.m. until nine p.m., and she usually showed up right as T was leaving, around two. If she wasn't there when T was ready to go, T would wait until she showed. Overtime paid extra, and all T had to do was sit there and wait. But apparently the owner noticed just how often that happened and hated paying T overtime. So Twee got fired, and the gravy train skidded off the track—not only would they lack Twee's regular hourly earnings, they wouldn't be getting T's overtime pay either, and every little bit counted now that there were just the three of them.

Twee pulled out her cage and went back to dragging it to the riverside to protest and collect donations. Every morning she was gone by seven and didn't come home until six-thirty so that she could be sure to catch the commuters both going to and coming from their jobs. For as long as she stayed out there in her cage, it didn't do much good—she almost never brought home more than a few dollars in change. Nobody seemed to care much what she was doing, and a girl in a cage wasn't such a disturbing spectacle anymore.

THE FIFTH OR SIXTH TIME the stuffed monkey toy seemed to wind itself up and rattle to life on its own was the last time any of them could take it. It happened when Kohl and T were leaning against the kitchen counter sharing a jug of water and licking the icing off a mocha doughnut Kohl had managed to find in the day-old bin at the doughnut place. They were torn between leisurely enjoyment of the doughnut and trying to finish it before Twee got home. Even though she'd told them she was fine with it, and she had started eating a little something every few days just to keep going, they both felt awkward and a bit guilty eating so decadent a thing in front of her. She looked like a skeleton with a little skin pulled over it. Her knees, her wrists, her ankles were knobs of bone that stretched her sallow skin and looked gigantic in comparison to the sticks of her arms and legs.

T passed the doughnut to Kohl and pushed back from the counter.

"Finish it," T said. "I'm done."

"Oh, gee, thanks! Finish this whole thing?" Kohl held up the nub of doughnut—less than a bite left, really—and then shoved it into her mouth. Around the doughnut she said, "I don't even know if I can eat this big bad doughnut all by myself! It's too much!"

"Adorable," T said. "Very attractive. You're so dainty."

"F you, jerk," Kohl said, laughing.

"Do you kiss Kevin with that mouth?"

"I do more than that."

"Stop. Please, stop," T said. "My ears are starting to bleed."

From the top of the fridge, where it had been put to guard the cigarettes, the monkey toy whirred and made some stop-start claps of the cymbals, then ground to a stop, glaring at them with a grotesque, toothy grin on its blank face.

"That is the creepiest, most horrifying, bone-chillingly awful nightmare of a thing in the entire world, and I would like to murder Twee for bringing it into our lives," Kohl said.

"I'm usually against violence," T said. "But I'm with you on that one."

Shuddering, Kohl threw the monkey in a cupboard and slammed the door closed so they didn't have to look at it, but every few minutes they could hear it whir to life and clomp its cymbals a few times. It was as though they'd locked a tiger in the cabinet—they could hear something predatory moving around in there and expected that, at any moment, the cupboard doors would swing open and the thing would come flying out at them.

"I can't take it anymore," Kohl said after half an hour of self-conscious attempts at conversation that didn't involve the monkey. "It's like that *Twilight Zone* with the ventriloquist's dummy." She stalked to the cabinet and pulled it open, then grabbed the lucky monkey and tucked it under her arm.

"What are you doing?"

Kohl reached up to the top of the fridge to grab a cigarette and tucked it behind her ear.

"Going out for a smoke."

"With that thing?"

"Two of us are going out," Kohl said. "But only one of us is coming back." She waggled her eyebrows and dropped the pack of matches into her pocket.

"I hope it's you," T said and shivered.

WHEN KOHL CAME BACK A few minutes later, she was monkeyless. Cold air and the burning smell of cigarette floated around her in a cloud, a strange combination of freshness and staleness that was familiar and comforting to T.

"It's done," she said. "You can calm down now."

"You sound like you just did a hit job for the mob or something."

"It was a little like that," Kohl smiled. "But he's out of our hair, officially."

"Not a moment too soon, since we have so little hair to spare." T caressed the shiny bald side of Kohl's head.

WHEN TWEE GOT HOME THAT night, T and Kohl were eating dinner, a gelatinous attempt at rice and beans about which Kohl was very sorry. They told Twee right away about the demise of the monkey toy. Kohl seemed almost proud.

"How could you do that without asking me?" Twee exclaimed. "I brought him in here! He was mine!"

"Yours?" Kohl said. "I thought we were working against that kind of property thing."

Twee flopped down on the bedding and stared at the ceiling. "You know exactly what I mean," she said.

"We had to get rid of the thing before it came to life and murdered us all in our sleep," T said. "It was creepy, and it was an awful reminder of our biggest mistake. We don't take things for ourselves, ever. I'm glad it's gone. I felt guilty every time I looked at it."

"Fine," Twee said, but it sounded as though it was anything but. She stared up at the ceiling in silence for several minutes. T and Kohl talked quietly about decidedly *not* the monkey while they ate forkfuls from the quivering mass of rice and beans in a pot between them.

"What did you do with him?" she finally asked.

"We took him to a farm upstate," Kohl said. Twee, despite herself, snorted.

"He was really bad luck," T said. "Bad things started happening as soon as he showed up."

"That's not true! You're being weirdly superstitious!" Twee said.

"Well, the monkey showed up just after you did, and bad things started happening and then everything fell apart right after, so it was either the monkey or it was you," Kohl said.

"Now it's *me*?" Twee shouted. "What the hell did I do to you?" Twee was struggling into a sweater as she shouted, and her voice came out all muffled.

"You brought the thing into our lives," Kohl said simply. "Things were fine until you showed up." T stomped a light warning on Kohl's foot, but she didn't seem to notice.

"Hey, now," T tried instead. "It's nobody's fault but Peebo and Vas. They're just jerks."

"Jerks we'd been dealing with just fine before," Kohl said.

Twee stood up and pulled a giant sweatshirt over her sweater—she looked like that advertisement guy made out of marshmallows, round and soft and slow-moving—then crammed her feet into the first pair of shoes she found by the door. They were actually T's, and they looked like clown shoes at the ends of Twee's scrawny legs. She clomped to the door.

"Maybe I should just get the hell out then?" Twee shouted.

"You said it; I didn't," Kohl said. "But now that it's on the table…"

"You're so nasty!" Twee said. "All I've been is nice to you, and you're so nasty to me! Your politics suck and you're a hypocrite." She yanked open the door and struggled out, then leaned back in and said, "I'll be back in an hour, if anyone cares!'

Kohl laughed, and it sounded cruel. "Some storm-out this is! Like a runaway little kid who's not allowed to cross the street! Leaving in a huff doesn't mean much if you come back! When you stalk out, you're supposed to go for good!"

"You should be so lucky," Twee shouted at Kohl, then turned to go. She walked with a shuffle, trying to keep the too-big shoes on her feet, and it made the whole exit less dramatic and more comical than she'd probably hoped.

Still, after she left, it felt as though a vacuum had sucked the air out of the room.

"That was mean," T said.

Kohl shrugged and ate another forkful of miserable beans and rice. "Doesn't mean it isn't true."

When Twee returned after an hour, sullen, slightly rain-damp, too quiet, Kohl didn't even look up from the papers on which she scribbled.

KOHL BEGAN TO LOOK HAGGARD. The hollows under her eyes took on a yellowish-purplish hue, as if she'd been punched and had developed two black eyes. Her skin paled. She bumped around the squat clumsily, as if she didn't even see the walls and counters and junk in her way, and thumped against things repeatedly like a moth caught inside and trying to get out. Her head was way elsewhere.

Sometimes, in the middle of the night, on the sleepy path to a midnight bathroom trip, T would come upon Kohl hunched over a notebook by the window, trying to scribble by the streetlight.

Finally, one night, after using the bathroom and on the way back to bed, T said, "What are you doing up? It's the middle of the night."

Kohl jumped, as if she'd not even heard T's noisy lumbering. "I'm just writing some stuff before I forget," she hissed. "Go back to bed."

They heard Twee moan groggily from the bedding on the floor, and T crept closer to Kohl so they could whisper.

"What stuff?"

Peering over Kohl's shoulder, T could see it looked like lyrics, with a few scratched chord notations, but it was too dim to make out any specifics. The light kept moving, thrown back and forth by the tree branch that swayed and scratched outside the window.

"It's nothing," Kohl whispered. "Just some music ideas. I get them when I relax enough, just as I'm falling asleep, and it wakes me back up. Just writing it down before I forget, then I'll be back to bed. Otherwise, I'll be thinking about it all night and I won't be able to sleep."

"You're writing music again? That's awesome." T's eyes itched, and the squat looked wavy and blurred in the dark. Kohl had clearly been there for a while and wasn't planning to go back to bed soon. She sat in the windowsill, feet propped against the corner of the wall and the window sash. She had a mug of something brown and soupy-looking that was probably coffee clamped between her knees and a notebook balanced against her thighs. Little hazy smears on the window where she'd rested her forehead were a trace of her concentration, like tracks through snow.

"Quiet!" Kohl whispered, cocking her head in the direction of Twee and the bedding on the floor. "And I'm not writing anything with you hovering over me, so go back to bed."

"Got it." T smooshed Kohl's cheeks between both hands before turning to go. "I'm so proud of you."

"Go. You're going to wreck it, and I'm going to lose my mojo soon."

141

"Right," T whispered and picked a careful path back to the bed. Twee grumbled and snuggled closer when T got in. She gripped T's side like a baby koala.

Without opening her eyes, she said, "What's that about? Is everybody okay?"

T put a hand over the back of Twee's skinny neck. "It's all fine; everything's really good. Sorry to wake you."

"What's wrong with Kohl?" Twee said, then sat up suddenly. The blankets fell away from her and she sat shivering in a white T-shirt and underwear, scrawny and so pale she almost glowed in the low light. She called hoarsely, "Kohl?"

"Shhh, don't," T said, chuckling and trying to cover where Twee's mouth probably was. It was hard to tell in the dark. "You're going to bug her, and then she won't be able to write. She's writing music. She's fine."

"Why is she composing at this time of night?" Twee asked testily, but it was only a half-awake question, and she dropped back to sleep before hearing an answer. Her breath—wet, a little sour—puffed against T's neck, getting slower and softer until it evened out.

T lay awake for a long time, pretending to sleep but watching Kohl's silhouette on the windowsill and listening to the scratch of her pen. *At least one of us is doing something real*, T thought, and was immediately clutched in disappointment. There wasn't even anything T was avoiding doing—that was part of the problem. T had nothing anymore, except an endless string of days in the churning, dusty hum of the laundromat. And it wasn't as if anything was in the way; no demands on time prevented T from writing that brilliant book or painting that glorious painting or... That was exactly the problem, T figured. *Nothing* filled in the blank. There was nothing, *nothing*, that T wanted to do anymore except to get by. T had spent so long thinking about how to keep going, keep safe, get through the winter, find a pair of shoes or enough food or clean water, there was no part of T left for thinking about or doing anything else. Getting by was hard enough; aside from that, there was nothing T needed to do, no urgent idea that called out in the middle of the night and just had to be captured before it slipped away.

It was a delicate moment, Kohl writing, quiet and alone, and T watching her from the other side of the room, wide awake and staring desperately into the dark just to make out the shape of her chewing the end of her pen, shifting her legs, bending her head low, and scribbling. They were in the same room, but in entirely different worlds. Entirely alone. T squinted through the dimness like a voyeuristic creep.

CHAPTER 10

THE STUFF LEFT AFTER ALL THE LAST STRAWS ARE GONE

T WOKE TO THE SMELL of coffee. Nothing ever got hot enough in the sink to make coffee that smelled like this. It wasn't sour and watery or thin and bitter; it smelled like roasting, like comfort.

When T emerged from sleep, Twee was in the kitchen, dancing from foot to foot. She had lined up three paper cups, the steam from which she was dramatically fanning in the direction of their bed.

"You're up!" she cried and abandoned the coffee long enough to throw herself at T. "Look what I got us!"

She was being far too loud—Kohl was still bundled under spare clothing in the heap of blankets on the floor; the slight shift of her hip as she breathed was the only indication that a person was under the pile.

T furrowed brows and said, in a significantly lowered voice, "Keep it down, or you're going to wake her."

"Too late." Kohl's voice rose from the heap. There was no movement to indicate they hadn't imagined it. Twee covered her mouth.

"I'm so sorry!" she stage-whispered. "I just was so excited, and you guys took forever to get up. Look what I got us!"

Twee fanned her hands over the coffee.

"I thought you were on a hunger strike," Kohl said, rising suddenly from under the pile. She looked like one of those old movie vampires levitating up from a coffin, stiff and swift, to scare the pants off some intruder. Kohl rubbed her face and what little hair was left on her head.

"I *am* on a hunger strike. But liquids don't count," Twee said. "You can have liquids."

"Even soup?" T said.

"Well, yeah," Twee said, her face pinched in thought. "I think so."

Kohl crawled out from under the clothing, letting it fall in clumps around her, and staggered to the counter. She wrapped her hands around one of the paper cups and pulled it against her chest, then bent her head and let the steam warm her face.

"This smells amazing," she said. "But we can't afford this kind of fanciness. We make coffee in the sink."

"Not today," Twee said. She pushed a cup toward T and took the last one for herself. "Today, we luxuriate in this. We relish. We revel. We *bask*." She clinked her cup against T's with an anticlimactic paper bump, then drank two large gulps.

"Wait. Even a *cream* soup?"

"Well. That's not really an option right now anyway," Twee said.

T sniffed the coffee, licked the rim of the cup, but did not drink right away. T felt leery of the luxury, coming, as it had, out of nowhere, with no effort or consideration on their part, but then decided it might be a gift of the universe that may as well be properly, gratefully enjoyed. There were worse sins than comfort and pleasure. Probably. Though comfort and pleasure seemed to be at the heart of a lot of really selfish behavior. But having the wonderfully warm coffee didn't mean someone else couldn't also enjoy a wonderfully warm coffee—it wasn't taking anything away from anybody else, really. Except T knew that wasn't exactly true. Everything had a price. Everything cost somebody something. Just ask the coffee bean pickers.

Kohl rapped a knuckle against T's forehead. "You home? Your face looks like you went to a bad place."

"Yeah, I guess I did," T said, shaking it off. "Guilt, is all. This just feels—"

"Too nice," Kohl finished.

Twee actually rolled her eyes.

"It's just a cup of coffee. You earned it. Relax," she said, taking another gulp.

"How *did* we earn it?" Kohl narrowed her eyes. "We can't afford stuff like this. We have a budget for food and water and stuff we actually *need*."

Twee looked proud, swelling up as if she'd pop if she didn't let out what was inflating her. She reached under her shirt and pulled out a dirty envelope, opening it wide so they could all see the stack of bills stuffed inside.

T couldn't help reaching out to run a finger over the edge of the stack. There had to be a couple hundred bills—even if they were all ones, that meant a lot of money. "How?"

Twee bowed and placed the envelope carefully on the counter between them. She held out her hands as though she'd just completed a card trick.

"My gift to the squat. No strings. We can keep some and give some to charity."

"How?" Kohl repeated T's question. Her voice was a razor.

Twee shrugged. "When I got fired, it sort of walked out with me, I guess."

"You *stole* that from the laundromat?" Kohl slammed her cup of coffee onto the counter. "This is stolen coffee, then?"

"If you want to think of it that way," Twee said. "The laundromat can afford it, and I figured we could give the money to people who needed it. And *we* need some, too, to keep the project going. It's like The Uproots."

"This is different," T said.

"How?" Twee said. She seemed genuinely confused.

Kohl had left the counter and was squatting by their bed, viciously pushing the tumble of clothes into a new pile that was no neater than the original mess but did, at least, take up less real estate. She shook her head, kept shoving clothes, keeping things moving but not making it any neater.

"How do you not see a difference?" she mumbled at the fabric. "It's completely not the same."

"We don't take *money*; we take *things*," T intervened.

"But it's the same, really," Twee said. "Possessions are possessions, no matter the form."

"As you seem to so keenly intuit, money buys possessions, but it also buys food and medical care. It buys a place to live. It buys electricity and water. People need food and doctors. They don't need blenders and TVs."

"Money isn't the root of all evil," T said. "Possessions are. Greed is different from need. We don't take money someone might need to get medicine or food."

Twee sighed. "But you can't ever know what they're going to use it for."

"Nope. Which is why we stay out of it," Kohl snapped.

"You're so self-righteous! You want everyone to know how perfect you are! It's all a show. You let your boyfriend buy you nice stuff; you just won't buy it yourself. It's all a show. You're a hypocrite!"

Kohl actually laughed, a cold, sharp sound. "*You're* telling *me* about putting on a show? The girl who sits in a dog cage and makes a public display of not eating? Okay."

"That's different!" Twee shouted. She'd curled her hands into fists, and every tendon in her neck seemed to be pulled taut. "I'm raising awareness! I'm making people think!"

"You're making people think you're an overprivileged fool for sitting in a dog cage on a sidewalk, sure. But I doubt it *does* anything real."

T listened to the furious volley between Kohl and Twee. The coffees were going cold, but nobody seemed to care. Twee smacked the counter with the palm of her hand, and that seemed to set her into very calm motion. She walked to the door, carefully pushed her feet into her shoes, and pulled a hat low over her head. She put her hand on the doorknob.

"At least I'm trying to talk to people instead of scaring them into doing what I want."

When Kohl didn't say anything, didn't even look up from the cup of coffee she was swirling and swirling, Twee added, "At least I try. All you do is criticize." She glared at Kohl. "Nothing's good enough for you. And T, you do nothing about it, just sit there like a statue of someone better than me, Buddha or someone. There's no such thing as neutrality, you know. You're both hypocrites." She looked pointedly at T, then opened the door and left.

"Well, that went well," Kohl said.

WHEN T WENT OUT, HOPING to find Twee at the river again, T noticed she'd left the dog cage folded up against the wall of the building's foyer. T dragged the thing up the stairs to the squat to keep it safe, just in case somebody thought about stealing it. T wanted it to be there for Twee when she returned.

She didn't come back that night—or the next, or the next.

WHEN KOHL MOVED OUT OF the squat, she did it as quickly and with as little fuss as she could manage. While T was at the laundromat, she stuffed her clothing into a garbage bag and took it to Kevin's, then circled back to the laundromat with a glazed doughnut and two cups of coffee. T and Kohl sat in the office, and for once Kohl took the busted swivel chair and left the good one for T, which should have been a dead giveaway.

"Okay, so, well, I'm moving in with Kevin. He asked me, and I said yes, mostly because I miss a hot shower and most of my stuff was there already, but I'm not abandoning you," she said in one breath.

"What?" T said. The quarters T was arranging into stacks spilled sideways across the grimy desktop.

"I'm not abandoning you," Kohl said.

"I heard that part. But you're moving in with The Stupendous Kevin?"

"Yes, but I'm not abandoning you. You're still my best friend, and I'm still going to bring you doughnuts at work and everything."

T scoffed. "How will that work, having a homeless best friend when you're living in the Stupendous Suburbs? You'll have a library card and a mailbox, and I'll have my pillow stuffed with newspapers, and we can get together for coffee I can't afford and talk about the good old days when we were starving and freezing *together*?"

"I already have a library card," Kohl said.

"Except I'll still be starving and freezing, just by myself."

"The good old days are really not that great, and I can't do it anymore."

The laundromat was yellowed and sour and dusty; T pushed the stacks of quarters away, letting them topple and spill across the desktop. A few fell and went rolling into the darkness under the desk.

"Is Kevin really *that great*, or are you just using him to get a hot shower on the regular?"

Kohl shut her eyes and clamped her mouth around an inhaled breath and held it all in until her skin grew purple and blotchy. She shook her head and scrubbed at her eyelids.

"You're being hurtful. I thought you'd be happy for me."

"By all means, grab what you can get for yourself. Never mind if other people can't have it. Why should that stop you from having everything you want?"

"I don't know what that means," she whispered. Her fingernails were digging into the palms of her hands, turning the skin nearly white.

There were a straggling few folks at the laundromat; mostly, they sat in the chairs by the front window and watched the TV. The blinging, happy siren sounds of *The Price Is Right* bubbled in the background. The Proper Old Lady sat in her usual spot by the window, waiting for her washer to finish churning, with her back straight, her hands folded carefully in her lap and a brown hat with a robin's-egg blue bow tilted just so over one eye. She was watching them carefully, averting her eyes every time T or Kohl looked her way. Nobody else looked up, even when T broke into frantically loud ranting.

"You don't know what that means? Of course you don't! It means not all of us can get married or move to the suburbs and have exactly what we want when things get too tough. It means not everybody can dupe some dumbass into taking care of them and fixing all their problems and then have the dumbass thank them for the privilege. It means some people have to live in the real world while other people get to run away and live in… in…"

"In a place that's nicer than they deserve," Kohl finished.

"That's not what I mean."

"It's true, though. I don't want to fight." Kohl looked sad, and T suddenly felt very tired.

Across the room, the Proper Old Lady coughed lightly into her gloved hand while staring pointedly at her knees.

"The consequences aren't the same for everybody, is all," T said more quietly after a moment.

"I know that. But it's not a scam. I know he's weird, but he's not just some dumbass. I think he's really that great," she said.

T's throat burned, and the metal bones of the broken chair pushed through the thin padding into T's thighs. There was no comfortable way to sit.

"Twee was right, you *are* a hypocrite."

Kohl didn't say anything, just scratched at a hole in the knee of her jeans and sniffed. The TV babbled. The jitter-hum of the washers and dryers, the street noise, the guy in the corner having a coughing fit, all of that sound pressed forward from the background to fill the gap of T and Kohl not saying anything.

"I have nobody left," T finally said. "I'm going to be completely alone now."

Kohl had been studiously ripping her empty paper coffee cup into smaller and smaller pieces, making a pile on the desktop. She took great pains to neaten the pile, stacking and restacking and squaring the edges. The pile bled little drops of coffee everywhere no matter what she did. It would never be neat.

A few of the pieces had a bright pink smear of lipstick on them. She picked up one of the pieces and worried it until her fingers were stained pink.

"You won't be alone. I won't let you be alone," she said.

T looked at her long and hard, then sighed. "But I am. Alone. Nobody's gonna fix that."

WHEN T GOT BACK TO the squat after work, Kohl's stuff was already gone, and there were two jugs of water, a loaf of bread and a note on the kitchen counter. T shoved the note into one of the cupboards without reading it. Kohl had left her dish and cup on the counter, but every other trace of her had disappeared.

Without the warmth of other people, the bed was cold and uncomfortable. Really, it was just a dirty lump of clothing and crumpled newspapers into which T burrowed to stay warm. The floor pressed up hard, the pile shifted and thinned with every movement, and it smelled. T noticed for the first time how shabby it really was: scant, tiny, a lonely little dot in the middle of a wide, filthy floor.

T's LIFE HAD ALREADY FELT small, but without anyone else in it, everything shrank to nearly nothing. At the squat, T recited off-the-cuff lines of iambic rhyming nonsense, clattered the pot in the sink, tapped the floor with a heel, all in order to make enough noise that the emptiness didn't feel so terrible. At the laundromat, T chatted with customers just to say something out loud and have someone else hear it.

On the third day, the Proper Old Lady came in. T had always thought she must be some fading, once-great lady easing into old age, always neat, always put together, only removing her fitted gloves to deal with the hardboiled egg she drew from the depths of her purse, laid carefully in the center of a napkin, and peeled and salted before eating.

"Excuse me, kiddo. Would you have change for a dollar?" The P.O.L. held out a crumpled dollar bill and smiled.

Up close, it was clear she'd slipped well past her former self and into the gentle struggle of lonely age. Her mouth was loose and dotted with a few remaining teeth. Her dress, her coat, her purse, all were fraying and ancient. Her hair was tucked tightly into a pilling knit hat. Her boots were covered in a dull film of mud; the leather was cracked and pocked with holes. The prim gloves were threadbare.

Nothing lasted.

T pushed a stack of quarters in her direction without reaching for the dollar she held out.

"Keep the dollar." T tried to smile kindly. "You're a regular. You should get a freebie once in a while."

The woman carefully folded the dollar and tucked it back into her purse.

"Thank you," she said, scooping up the quarters.

"Do you need any help? I'm good at folding," T said.

The woman widened her eyes and looked scandalized. "No. Thank you, though. I'm washing my skivvies today."

T couldn't help laughing. The P.O.L. winked.

"I'm Bert," she said, holding out a gloved hand.

"You can call me T." T took her hand and tried to do something more proper than a shake—a little squeeze and a tip upward—but it felt a touch smarmy. Bert didn't seem to mind.

"It's Roberta, I suppose, if we're being proper like *that*," she babbled, "but *Roberta* sounds too formal for me, and Bertie sounds too crass. So Bert it is."

"It suits you." T got the impression Bert didn't get the chance to talk to many folks either. Too many words seemed to tumble out of her at once, as if she was worried the chat would be limited and she needed to squeeze as many words as she could into the brief opportunity.

"T," she said. "It's nice to meet you, T. It's nice to put a name to that lovely face of yours. I see you every week, always sitting there, always working. You look much more interesting than most of the folks in this joint. I'm glad to meet you."

That should have ended the conversation, but Bert stood and beamed a near-toothless smile that T couldn't resist.

"Would you like to sit in the office with me and have some coffee? I just got some fresh, and I have an extra cup."

Bert's mouth formed a small, silent *oh*, and she put her hand on her chest. "Lovely, yes, coffee and good company! But where's your girlfriend?"

T's heart sank—every time things were going along nicely, something like this cropped up. People just couldn't let it ride—they had to figure out if T was a boy or a girl, and whether T had a boyfriend or a girlfriend, and what it all meant. Usually, at least, they did it nicely, like Bert; subtly, politely. But it still hurt, a frequent sting, like a papercut or a worm boring into a soft spot.

The disappointment must've shown on T's face because Bert waved her hand and said, "You know, the pretty one who comes in sometimes. The one with the doughnuts. Your friend, that pretty girl."

T nearly grabbed the poor woman and kissed her. It didn't take much nowadays to win T over—all you had to do was *not* be a jerk. T opened the half door to let Bert behind the counter, then quickly wheeled up the good chair and held it for her as she sat.

"That's probably Kohl," T said. "She's away for a while." T didn't want to get into a whole thing and left it at that.

"Well," Bert said, "I hope she's doing fine, but since she's away, there's space for me, so let's call it lucky." She set her purse carefully on the counter between the stacks of quarters and folded her hands on her knee. "Now, let's find out about you, T. Tell us everything, and don't leave out the good stuff."

She winked again, and T was thoroughly charmed.

T AND BERT SHARED COFFEE from the cup T had brought to work. Bert sat with T well past the point when her laundry had stopped whirling and as she left the office, while carefully pulling those prim gloves back on, she said, "This has been a true delight. What a lovely person you are, T."

She held out her hand, but this time gripped T's hand in return and pulled T forward, quickly squashing them both into a powdery-smelling hug.

"Are you here tomorrow?"

BERT VISITED MOST DAYS THAT week, just to sit with T. At first she brought her usual handful of clothes, which T suspected didn't need cleaning, and put them in the washer for a go-round; but she quickly let go of the excuse and simply appeared, brandishing a few candied fruit jells or a delicate piece of semolina cake wrapped in a handkerchief.

When T thanked her and offered a seat in the office, each time as if it were the first, Bert blushed and waved and said, "A little treat from the Turkish place near my home," and took the seat.

T began to bring two cups of coffee to work.

T DREADED GOING BACK TO the empty squat, where it was dark, where the space was too large, where the halls echoed with strange sounds but the squat itself was too quiet to bear. After a week, a red and white sign appeared on the front of the building. It said, "FOR SALE OR LEASE." Someone had taped a clear plastic tarp over the broken front window, and T had to carefully peel up a side just to get in and out. Three days later, T returned home to find the plastic sheeting had been replaced with newly glazed glass, and it looked as though someone had begun cleaning out the whole building. A long dumpster in front of the place was filled with debris—broken wood beams, plaster chunks, everything that had been inside. T dug a bit and found the dog cage and a couple pieces of nearly ruined clothing but left behind the broken bowls and piles of blankets (now covered in plaster dust and ripped beyond rescue) and hauled the few saved things back to the laundromat.

Closed, its machines silent and gaping empty, the laundromat was chilly, and its bleach smell was sharper. T didn't dare turn the lights on, but at least there was a bathroom and four walls. T stuffed the handful of clothes in a desk drawer, pulled an abandoned towel out of the Lost and Found bin, and curled up with it under the desk to sleep.

THE SUN WOKE T WELL before the laundromat had to be opened. T tossed the dirty clothes into a washer, patted clean with wet paper towels, and unlocked the front door.

It was a strange day. The light was eerily storm-colored, a glowing gray. Flat, dense clouds rushed overhead and made the air darken and lighten every other moment as if someone were flicking the lights. Rain splattered the windows and hissed in the gutters. Nobody, not a soul, came into the laundromat until afternoon, so the machines and the television were blissfully silent. In the new quiet, the world outside and all its noise pressed in, filling the little place with honk and splash and motor and shout.

T combed the phone book for somewhere to stay—the laundromat would only work for a day or two, and then another attendant would come in from a shift and notice T sleeping under the desk. All the shelters were either men-only or women-only places. T figured the women's shelter would be safer but decided to try both.

After work, T took the bus and visited the shelters. Neither would let T stay.

"This is for *women only*," the lady at the second place said. She sat behind the mottled bulletproof plastic window and refused to buzz the door open for T. "I wish I could help you, honey, but you need to go to the *men's* shelter on Fifth Avenue." She spoke slowly, with heavy articulation, as if she thought T was a child or hard of hearing. "The women here need a *safe space*."

The woman scooped her hair up on top of her head and snapped a red elastic band around the mass, signaling she would brook no argument and give T no more attention. She hadn't been unkind, not outright, but it felt that way when T pushed the front door open and stepped onto the street. It was still cold and shimmering wet, now evening-dark and crowded.

T tried the family shelter, the only place that took both men *and* women, but they had no space left. Besides, the lady told T, they didn't *accommodate* single people anyway. The place was for *families.*

T walked the long walk back to the laundromat, the acrid smell, the lint and grime, the rickety chairs, and the office in shambles. Under the desk it was dirty and wet from dragged-in rain, and even with the wall to lean against, even after a long hour of deliberate concentration, T felt adrift, unmoored, exposed and sleepless.

Everyone was gone now, off to better things, dry homes with locked doors and warm showers and familiar people and gentle yellow light and soft beds. Kohl and Peebo and Vas and even probably Twee were right where they wanted to be, *safe as houses.* The phrase made so much sense. Everyone in the world was safe tonight, safe as houses.

Everyone except T.

T was the one not safe as houses, not even close to a house, never mind a home. T was the one left holding the proverbial bag of consequences of The Uproots' work, too. The breaking-and-entering trial stood tall and opaque, like a metal wall against the murky future. The slab of desktop overhead was a heavy rock waiting to crash down. Twee's dog cage still leaned against the wall in the corner, unclaimed. T shook it open and crawled inside.

T SLEPT IN THE CAGE for two nights. On the second morning, finally, the laundromat was full and noisy as usual. The P.O.L.—Bert— showed up with a handkerchief-wrapped stash of tangerine slices and presented it like a tiny treasure. Their fingers shining with juice, T and Bert hunkered over the desk in the office and ate the tangerine together.

"This is so great, Bert, I really needed this. Thank you." T licked the juice from each fingertip.

Bert dotted at her lips and palms with a napkin. She seemed to take pleasure in everything being *just so*. She smiled.

"It's been gray and rainy lately," she said. "We all need a little color now and then, I think. Hilton used to say that."

"Hilton? Your husband?" T asked.

Bert snorted, uncharacteristically unladylike. "Good god, no! Hilton? My *brother!* Good god!"

"I'm so sorry. I wasn't suggesting that you—"

"The man was a pig!" she laughed. "Even if he wasn't my brother, he would never be my type!" She fanned herself in mock horror, then covered her mouth and shook her head. "What did I say? Don't get me wrong, I've never even considered it!"

T laughed, then asked for more stories, and Bert talked about Hilton: a painter, a slob, a good cook, an opinionated jerk; everything in his messy apartment was covered in gobs of paint and spilled coffee.

"You always had to wash a glass before you drank out of it," she said, "or you'd be drinking purple water before you knew it. Once, I poured myself some orange juice and found a giant glob of gesso in the bottom *after* I drank the whole glass. Every time I left his place, I'd have to scrub at least one of my articles with turpentine. You couldn't sit on anything unless you wanted to get *embellished.*"

Hilton had died three years ago. Bert had come upon him in his room, splayed out across the table, a glass of something cheap and awful-smelling still clutched in his hand.

"It smelled like turpentine, so they thought it was a suicide," Bert said. "Maybe it wasn't. It could have been gin. That man was a drinker. The window was wide open. The cats were gone, and he had frozen to death. His skin was gray."

Her voice wavered at that, and she stopped speaking. T put both hands over hers and squeezed. Bert looked grateful, but as if she'd break apart if T did one more gentle or kind thing, so T squeezed again and leaned back, letting their hands drop.

"I'm sorry," Bert said. She stabbed at her cheeks with the handkerchief that had held the oranges, and the gesture was so unexpectedly careless, so *messy*, T's throat clenched. T rooted in the drawer for the tissues and handed her the near-empty box.

"Thank you," she said, taking one. "I'm sorry."

"Bert, stop."

"I just miss him, I think. And in my memory, whenever I try to think of him, he's *gray* and *stiff* and just not *him*."

"That's a horrible memory."

Bert nodded and pressed the tissue clump to the corner of her eye. "What a silly old lady I'm being, ruining a lovely afternoon. What a fuss."

T didn't answer her; she seemed determined to apologize, embarrassed by the slip of humanity in front of T, as if T had seen her skivvies after all.

Bert sniffed. "What's that? Do you have a dog in here?"

Bert was pointing to the cage, which T had neglected to disassemble. A lump of towels sat in its center like an accusation.

"No, not exactly," T said.

"Not exactly?"

"Not at all, I guess. It belonged to a friend. I've sort of taken it over."

"What?" Bert said.

It was, T figured, a rather inevitable response. T sighed. "It's mine now," T said. "I've been using it for naps."

"You what?" Bert's hand was on her chest again in that ridiculous gesture of genteel horror she liked to affect. "Tell me you do not sleep in there!"

T shrugged. "Better than under the laundry table?"

"Child, aren't you afraid someone will *rob* the place while you're unconscious and locked with a towel in a dog cage?" She sniffed. "I cannot believe I just had to say that to another person. You *are* a person. Not an animal."

"I don't *lock* it," T said, because Bert seemed to be expecting a response. Bert looked horrified, so T added, "Besides, I only sleep in there after closing. The front door is locked."

T quickly realized too much had been said when Bert looked even more horrified, but by then it was too late to go back. "Are you living here?" she asked.

"Lately," T said sheepishly.

After Bert had properly vented her astonishment and alarm at this, she refused to leave for the rest of the afternoon. T was fairly certain she intended to stay there until closing in order to supervise. When the last launderer had left and the machines were still, Bert remained.

"I've decided that you will come home with me tonight. You will sleep on my couch," she stated.

"Bert, I'm quite fine right here," T lied.

"You are absolutely not quite fine. You need a good place to sleep comfortably, and I have a couch where you can do just that. It's not safe, sleeping on the floor of a laundromat. What if someone catches you? And I am sure there are rats."

T had no argument and so, when the laundromat had been locked down for the night, T followed the P.O.L. to the bus stop and then to the crooked blue house in which she lived.

INSIDE, DAINTY LAMPS WITH BRONZE stems and blue glass shades glowed away the dark. A nubbly green carpet was worn in paths from the front door to the fat, doily-strewn sofa, and from the sofa to the kitchen door. The windowsills, a bookcase, and several small side tables spilled over with ceramic figurines that jittered together with a low tinkling rattle every time a car drove by.

Bert took T to the kitchen, gestured toward a spindly chair at the table, and put a kettle on the stove. She prattled as it boiled and, when it whistled, she filled a teapot and set it between them on the table.

The table was already laid with two flowered teacups, two saucers and spoons, two napkins, a dish of sugar. It was as if she'd been expecting T—or someone—to join her.

When she saw T's raised eyebrows, she said, "For Elijah." When T still didn't seem to understand, she added, "The empty seat at the table. It's for Elijah."

"Is that another brother?"

That really made her laugh: a breathy, creaky sound that was somehow still pleasant. She dropped a spoonful of sugar into her cup and stirred.

They sipped their tea without speaking much. Every few minutes, the figurines in the outer room made their shaking clinks. When they'd finished, they took their cups to the sink, where T delighted in washing them with warm running water and a real sponge while Bert busied herself in the outer room, spreading sheets and blankets over the couch so T could sleep there.

"Thank you, Bert," T said when Bert laid a towel across the arm of the couch.

"It's a bit old, but it still dries you off!" she said cheerfully.

"I didn't mean that," T said. "Thank you for all this."

Bert waved it off. "No bother! It's nice to have another person around. You'll keep me company."

AFTER TWO DAYS, T CAME home to find a new pillow on the couch.

"I don't have a guest room," Bert apologized, "but I won't have you camping, either. If you're staying here for a while, let's make it as nice as we can, shall we?"

The next day, Bert left T a pair of wool gloves. The day after, three pairs of socks.

"Bert, you can't afford all this, and I don't need all these gifts!" T told her when, the next day, T returned home from the laundromat to find that a new brown leather wallet had appeared on the couch.

"It's nothing! I'm just trying to help you get what you need. I can afford this, where I shop."

Bert toddled into the kitchen before T could respond. T followed her, still holding the wallet in case it was needed as an exhibit in the upcoming argument. But Bert simply put a kettle on the stove, hummed, and scrubbed invisible stains off the counter as she waited for the water to boil.

While Bert filled the teapot, T cleaned and set out the two teacups and saucers. The task had become so habitual that T barely noticed doing it. They sat together at the kitchen table, right where they always seemed to sit, and Bert poured them each a cup.

She stirred and stirred her evening tea intently. The silence was long. T looked at her sideways, so Bert left the table to shake a small rug and let the dust fly out the door. She seemed always to be cleaning something. She dusted the figurines every day. It was almost as if she had the figurines simply to have something to dust.

Bert beat the rug against the door frame a few times, then let it flutter back into place on the kitchen floor. She dropped back into the chair at the table, winded.

"That takes it out of me," she said, fanning herself. "I need a rest."

"Let me do those things next time," T said. "Where do you shop?"

"I firmly believe one should clean one's own house. That's not something you can ask another person to do. It's my dirt; I'll tend to it." She blotted her forehead with the handkerchief. T had no idea where she kept it, but she seemed to manifest it wherever she was, whenever she needed it.

"But *I'm* staying here now, too, so some of it is *my* dirt. And really, where do you shop?"

"What? Groceries at the Giant Eagle. Dresses at the Goodwill. Why?"

"You said things are affordable where you shop, and I'd like to check it out myself."

"Oh!" Bert laughed and held up a hand, fingers wiggling. "Not available to you, probably. I get a discount."

"Senior discount or something?"

She leaned over and swatted T on the arm. "You shush! Disrespect!"

T mustered the hardest look possible and trained it on Bert. Bert relented and held up her hand again.

"If you must know, T, I give myself the discount. Five-finger discount."

"You *stole* these socks?"

"Serves them all right for being bigots about age. They don't even see an old lady like me. They only care about young folks. You young folks have got the money."

T had to laugh at the irony of that, sitting in the P.O.L.'s well-appointed kitchen in the cozy home she owned, sleeping on her couch and not even a proper bed to T's name.

"So you're stealing from them?"

"I'm teaching them. It's an object lesson in humanity. If they learn to see me, then I can't take from them, can I?"

T shrugged and set the saltshaker spinning on its side. "Visibility isn't everything, you know."

The P.O.L. chuckled again. "Listen, it's a no-win situation. Young women always get watched, whistled at, evaluated, sized up, checked out. You get your cheeks pinched—both kinds, I mean." She patted her rear. "You get tired of being looked at all the time. Sometimes you just wish people would leave you alone. Everyone is busy keeping an eye on what you do, how much you eat, where you go, who you go *with*."

Bert raised her eyebrows significantly. T turned and turned the teacup in its saucer, not sure if Bert was talking about T or herself.

"But when you get old—" Bert banged the table suddenly, and T jumped, "you turn invisible, and sometimes a person can feel bad about it. I'm sure you know about that."

It was the first time Bert had broached the subject with T, and it made T wonder. T had always assumed Bert simply didn't notice T's difference—maybe she assumed T was a girl, or a boy, and didn't question it. But now T wondered if Bert actually saw things more clearly than that and what Bert saw just didn't make a difference to her at all.

"People always want to be *seen,*" Bert said. "But invisibility has its power, too, kiddo."

CHAPTER 11

THE BROKEN P.O.L.

THEY TURNED THE SITTING ROOM into a bedroom for T and spent most of their time chatting at the kitchen table. T didn't have much anyway, though Bert continued to pilfer little gifts and the cache of T's possessions grew. Most days, when T came home, a new thing was waiting, always something small enough to fit in Bert's purse but necessary enough to make a difference for T.

T stayed with Bert for a quiet and happy two weeks before something went wrong. T woke that Wednesday morning to shouting.

"T! T!" Bert was yelling. "T, help!"

T went running to Bert's room, but just before throwing the door open, T heard her panicked voice. "Close your eyes!" she rasped. "Come help me but close your eyes!"

Eyes closed, T threw the door open and went stumbling into the room. T had never been inside the room and didn't even know where anything was by which to navigate. Immediately, T tripped over some table or chair. "I can't help you *and* keep my eyes closed," T said, standing up. "I have to see where I'm going. Are you okay?"

T's eyes opened on a pretty awful scene. Bert was on the floor next to her bed. She was naked; her papery skin was flushed red. She'd tried to pull the sheets over herself but had only gotten them partway off the bed in a twisted, flowered mass that she used to cover her lap. One arm clamped across her chest. The other arm was revoltingly bent under her back. Her lips were quivering.

"Oh my god, Bert, what happened?" T dropped down and gently helped her ease the bent arm out from under her back. She yelped and whimpered. The wrist was purple and rubbery.

"Fell," she croaked.

"I'm going to call the ambulance. Where's the phone?"

"No phone," she said.

"You don't have a phone for emergencies? You're alone!"

"I've got you," she said.

T stood up. "I'm going out to the pay phone at the Giant Eagle. I'll be back quick." Then T added, rather needlessly, "Stay right here."

Just as T turned to run out, Bert grabbed T's ankle and said, "No."

"Bert, we need the ambulance. I think you've broken your arm. Who knows what else."

"Please. I need clothes."

"I don't think it's a good idea to move you right now," T said. "What if something else is broken?"

Bert started to cry, so T gave in and found the loosest dress in the closet and tried to help her pull it on. She couldn't move her arm without sobbing, so T fetched her dressing gown instead and simply wrapped that around her and tied the belt without putting the broken arm into the sleeve. She was so thin; T tried not to notice the ribs pressing through the loose skin, the soft, slack breasts, the delicately creped throat. Everything on Bert looked so heartbreakingly fragile. The robe created a makeshift sling, binding her arm against her chest in a way that seemed perhaps a little more comfortable.

Even so, Bert was sweating and holding her breath. She was shaking.

"I'm okay, it's okay, let's just get it done," she muttered through gritted teeth when T looked concerned.

T and Bert worked together to get her untwisted and sitting, leaning against the side of the bed. Bert sighed and let her head fall back. Her breath was heaving.

"I'll be right back," T said. "I'm going to call an ambulance."

"Okay," Bert whimpered.

UPON RETURNING, T LEFT THE front door open and curled up next to Bert on the floor by her bed. She didn't speak, just let her head drop onto T's shoulder. Every moment or two, T heard her sniffle. T tried to take even breaths in order to soothe her with the rise and fall of the shoulder on which she leaned. T thought of salt wind and sand grit, the ebb and flow of air in and out. A kind of ocean rhythm.

When the ambulance arrived, the EMTs called through the open front door. T loped out to greet them and guide them to Bert. They got her onto a gurney and into the ambulance with only a few whimpers from Bert. They said T couldn't ride in the ambulance but would have to get there some other way. Luckily, the hospital was less than a mile away; T ran.

T found Bert in the E.R., moved to one of the curtained-off cubicles where they stored the patients. She was groggy—they'd obviously given her something—and tearstained. When T slipped in through the curtains, Bert brightened and looked as if she'd just won the lottery.

"Oh, *you!*" she said. They'd definitely given her something. "I thought you'd gone home!"

"I would never!" T said, pulling the one available plastic chair near her bedside. "They wouldn't let me ride in the ambulance, so I ran."

"You're so young and fit! What a lovely surprise!" Bert gripped T's arm with her good hand. The other arm was reddish-purple and swollen. It looked absolutely awful.

"I've really messed up my arm somehow," Bert said. "I don't think we'll be going out anytime soon."

T chuckled and nodded. "Probably not, Bert. You okay?"

"They gave me medicine, and it is the most wonderful invention!" she said. "We should put in a call to Timothy Leary."

"You are looped out of your gourd," T said.

"Yes, it's very nice!" She sighed and closed her eyes. "But it's making me so tired."

"Why don't you rest? I'm not going anywhere. I'll be right here when you need me." T smoothed the coverlet across Bert's hips. She was so thin and bony that her body barely made a lump under the blanket.

"You're a good egg," she said and closed her eyes. She was quiet. T could hear the beeps and clanks coming from behind the neighboring curtains. Shoes squeaked on the polished floors outside. A man in the next cubicle droned on and on in a low hum. T couldn't tell if he was a patient, a visitor, or a doctor.

After a few moments, Bert began to speak, a dribble of words dropping from the corner of her mouth. She kept her eyes closed.

"Do you remember," Bert asked, "when we started The Klatch? We were just so clever, all of us. Jillian and Marta, plus Danna and Anna. Those girls were always together. I used to call them Danana, just one word like that, like banana. And you, you were there, I remember."

"I wasn't there," T said quietly, even though Bert didn't seem to want an answer.

"Just the six of us. Do you remember when we mooned Drew Lewis?"

T perked up. "No!"

"Oh, yes, that boob. We all went into his governor rally, remember, and we wore our nicest dresses and little white gloves and hats, proper girls, and when he got up there to speak, we all flipped up our skirts and showed him our bare bottoms!"

"You did not!" T wished so badly for a tape recorder or a witness or something to record the evidence of this conversation. Bert was always so proper, T had a strong feeling that once the painkillers wore off and Bert was her usual self, she'd deny everything.

"Oh yes, we did! I kept yelling, 'An ass for an ass!' but they didn't arrest me. They took everybody else except me. I kept yelling, but they didn't take me. They just ushered me out."

"Why did they take everybody else but you?" T asked.

Bert opened her eyes and gave T a steely look. "You've got to be kidding me. You *know why.* I was the nice white girl in the group. I wore a bra, you know, and a pink dress, and my hair was done up with a little pink hat like Jackie O, and they didn't assume I was a homosexual like Banana. They had no interest in me. I had to take up a collection from our friends just to bail everybody out. It was a fiasco. And that rat bastard Lewis still won."

T stroked Bert's hair and listened to the machines beep on the other side of the curtain. It was a strange thing to be in a place with no windows, no way to tell time at all. Shoes continued to creak by on the linoleum outside the curtain, but nobody came in.

"Oh, it *hurts* again, so much," Bert said, and tried to lift her arm. She looked at it when it wouldn't move. "It's so *heavy*! Is that mine?"

T laughed again. "The hand? Yes, it's yours. It's on your arm, after all."

"It doesn't look like mine," Bert said, clearly confused. "It's not the right shape or color. My gloves won't fit." She frowned. T handed her the paper cup of water from the metal counter near the gurney.

"No, probably not. Drink this. We'll get you new ones for now, but your hand will get smaller again, I promise. This is all temporary."

"Drink me, eat me," Bert said. "Okay, Caterpillar. I mean Shessshhh-ire Cat. Chess-ire. *Cheshire*."

She obediently sipped the water from the cup, then handed the cup—still practically full—back to T. She shook her head, then put her hand to her lips as if she was trying to keep the water from spewing out. T sighed and put the cup back on the counter.

"Do you want me to go find someone to come help you right now?"

"No, don't go!" Bert cried. "Stay a while. I'm just going to close my eyes for a minute."

Bert sank back onto the under-stuffed pillow. Her eyes were already closed—they'd hardly opened during their conversation—but T figured she meant to take a nap. Bert's mouth relaxed as she drifted.

"You're a good egg," she mumbled again. "You remind me of Telly."

T wanted to ask who Telly was and why T reminded Bert of him. Or her. Of Telly. But Bert had passed out and gone slack, so T sat and listened to the hum and beep of the E.R., the shuffling past of rubber-soled shoes, the whisk of curtains, the rumble of forced air from the vents.

T must have waited an hour before someone slid back the curtain and strolled in.

"Okay," the man said loudly, clearly in an effort to wake Bert.

She fluttered to life. "Oh! Hello, Doctor!"

The man seemed awfully young to be a doctor—pale, with a tuft of blond hair that floated above his scalp as if he'd just been shocked. He took a ballpoint pen from his pocket and clicked it several times before beginning to write on a clipboard.

"What happened to us here?" he said.

"I don't know what happened to *you*," Bert said, "but *I* fell getting out of bed and seem to have broken my wrist." She indicated the red and purple swollen lump at the end of her arm. "If, indeed, that is actually mine. There has been some debate."

The doctor forced a tight smile. "Well, let's just make sure it's actually broken. Sometimes you can sprain it and it feels like it's broken."

He tried to pick up her arm by the wrist, using his thumb and finger like a claw or a caliper. Bert yelped, and the doctor jumped back.

"I think that may just be broken after all. We'll take pictures to be sure, then get you mended up and home in time for soap operas."

Bert shot T a pained expression. "X-rays are probably more effective than pictures, don't you think?"

"Well," the doctor said absently. He continued to scribble on the clipboard. "Yes, of course."

"What she really needs to know," T said, "is whether she'll be able to fire a gun anytime soon. She's left-handed, and we have a couple heists coming up."

The doctor raised his eyebrows, then cleared his throat. He actually said, "Ahem."

Bert said, "It's just a .22, if that makes a difference."

THE DOCTOR BREEZED OUT AS quickly as he'd entered.

"Ass," Bert said.

They took her to have X-rays of the swollen limb, which confirmed she'd broken her wrist. T waited as the doctor, who didn't speak a word to them the whole while, wrapped her wrist in a splint.

"Doesn't she need a cast if it's broken?" T asked.

"You'll need to go to the clinic to get this set tomorrow, as soon as you can," he said. And then he patted her knee. "Get better soon!" he called as he left.

When the nurse came in several minutes later, she came with forms and pamphlets and a prescription that they had to get filled at the pharmacy as soon as possible, because it was a painkiller and Bert was probably really going to want it in about an hour. The nurse leaned over Bert, inadvertently brushing her with a massive set of breasts, to adjust and rewrap Bert's splint.

"That better?" she asked.

"You are an absolute angel. Why aren't you the doctor here?" Bert said, caressing the woman's cheek. Bert was incredibly fun when she was drugged.

"Doctors don't ever get the splints on right," she said, shaking her head. She left without answering Bert's question—she probably thought it answered itself—and then they were allowed to leave.

T took Bert home and got her settled in bed. Filling the prescription was going to be another problem, but Bert was starting to whimper again and T couldn't see her in pain. T had a little roll of cash saved from the laundromat—expenses had shrunk while living with Bert—but it probably wasn't enough to pay for the prescription. Tylenol or something would have to do.

On the street, the air had turned blue-gray without the sun; they'd been in the emergency room for the whole day. T hopped the bus and rode to the pharmacy but fell asleep on the ride home and missed the right stop. It took another bus ride—almost forty-five minutes—to get back to Bert's place.

When T returned, Bert was sleeping soundly, and T decided not to wake her just to give her medicine that would put her to sleep. Instead, T took the opportunity to look through Bert's house for a phone number or address, some way to contact Bert's family. T felt awful going through Bert's things as she slept—the woman was so proper and guarded her privacy so carefully, T knew she would have felt the search an affront had she been awake to see it.

T went through the entire house—closets, drawers, even under the bed—but found little. There were four dresses in the closet, two place settings of dishes in the kitchen cupboards, two pairs of shoes lined up neatly by the door, but nothing helpful: no phone numbers, no address book, no photographs, no evidence of family at all. T found one badly creased photograph of a man in baggy trousers with sideswept brown hair. T figured it was probably Hilton. Maybe Telly. T wasn't sure. On the bathroom counter, T found a hairbrush. It had been cleaned so carefully, there was only a single hair wound into its bristles. It looked as though Bert cleaned it every night. T placed it carefully, along with a glass of water and the bottle of Tylenol, on the bedside table near Bert's sleeping back, where she might find them in the morning.

IN THE MORNING, T CHECKED on Bert—still sleeping soundly, the splinted hand still resting like a gift on the pillow beside her head. T left a note with emphatic instructions about pill dosage, then decided not to leave the whole bottle just in case and instead to mete out a single dose and leave it by the note. T put the bottle with the rest of the pills high in a kitchen cupboard, where Bert would never accidentally find them. The clinic would have to wait until T got back from work—skipping work another day at the laundromat would definitely get T fired. In the meantime, T hoped, Bert would sleep most of the day.

The laundry only saw stragglers that morning—perhaps only twelve people came in—so T decided to close the doors at five and run home to Bert. On the way, T lifted a small clutch of pink carnations from a bucket outside the grocery store—the cheapest thing they seemed to have, so T tried not to feel terrible about stealing it—and ran the remaining few blocks to Bert's house.

BERT WAS STILL SLEEPING, SO T rattled her awake, got her stuffed into the loosest dress in the closet (Bert had to go without "underpinnings" because she couldn't put them on herself and wouldn't let T help), buttoned her into a coat and tied a kerchief over her hair—apparently not to her standard, because Bert slapped at T's hands and fumbled with the scarf one-handed until she was satisfied. They went out the door, and T toddled her through the rain to the bus.

"I feel like I have a couple of bowling balls rolling around inside my dress with no brassiere," Bert said.

"Hardly," T laughed.

"Well, bananas, at least," Bert said as T settled her onto the bench at the bus stop. T snorted.

"Cherries?"

"You should always be on drugs. This is fun," T said.

"Shush!" Bert hissed and swatted T's arm, even though there seemed to be nobody on the street for blocks. Light rain smattered the windshields of parked cars and made a chilly mist; the street looked ghostly. "I am not on drugs! Those are *prescription!*"

"Not even. It's just Tylenol. You never did drugs? Not even in your wild '60s days?"

"I am still in my sixties," Bert said, scowling.

"*Nineteen*-sixties," T said. "And you are *not* still in your sixties. You told the nurse at the hospital exactly how old you are."

"I did what? How old did I say?" Bert's face had stretched into a picture of alarm. One-handed, she had neglected her usually exacting makeup job, so she lacked both drawn-on eyebrows and the careful eyeliner that distinguished her fading eyes from her fading cheeks. Even without that emphasis, T could see that her lips bowed down and her forehead had acquired several wrinkles. Her expression was clear.

"I'll never tell." T squeezed her arm. Bert laughed and huddled closer to T on the metal bench. The glass bus shelter did little to shut out the wet as they waited.

"WHO WAS TELLY?" T ASKED.

They'd been admitted into the clinic and, after a long wait in the linoleum-and-plastic waiting room, had been tucked into a smaller curtained-off room to wait for someone to see them. Bert had been hoisted onto an exam bench, and her feet dangled a good six inches above the floor. She looked like a child, the way she was letting her legs swing. T wondered why medical places for poorer folks never seemed to bother with walls. Everything was always curtains, which shut out little and could be snapped open without warning. Walls and privacy seemed to be a privilege of the wealthy.

"We have been waiting in here interminably," Bert grumbled. "I have begun to believe they will never come in."

T sighed. "Who was Telly?"

"Telly?" Bert said, as if she hadn't heard.

"Right, Telly," T said. "You mentioned a Telly the other day, and you laughed at me when I asked if Telly was another brother, but you never actually said who Telly was, or is, or anything."

"Telly was my best friend," Bert said. "Teodora. She lived with me back a long time ago."

Bert didn't seem to want to speak more about it. She pressed her lips together and sniffed.

"Was she part of the Klatch?" T asked.

Bert's eyes widened. "You should know! She *started* the Klatch! Where is your history?"

Bert knocked her heels against the examination table on which she sat. *She must be irritated,* T thought, *because under normal circumstances she would never be so uncareful with her shoes.* Everything she owned was old, was worn, but lovingly cared for. Bert was one of those people who cared for everything.

T remembered visiting grandparents as a small child. T's grandmother had had a deck of playing cards she'd gotten on the single plane ride she'd taken in her entire life—those cards were precious. T's grandmother Bhavani would spread a cotton cloth across the table before removing the cards from their box and spreading them out to play a slow, careful game of solitaire. Before putting the cards away in their box, she'd use the corner of the cloth to wipe each one free of fingerprint. It took more time to set up and put away the cards than it did to play with them.

"Teodora is an activist," T said, mostly to prompt.

"She *was* an activist. Telly's gone," Bert said. Before T could ask anything more, someone called, "*Knock knock!*" and pulled the curtain aside before either of them could answer.

"We've got a broken wrist, I hear!" the kid said cheerfully. He was even younger than T, and he didn't seem to be doing much to try to look any older. He wore clean white sneakers and let his hair frizz into a thick reddish cloud that flopped over one eye. Still, the white coat gave him an air of officiality, and T felt the urge to respect it.

"*I* do," Bert grumbled. "You don't have to sound so excited about it."

The kid, to his credit, laughed and apologized. "Lucky for me, my wrists are okay. I'm Dr. Nolan, but you can call me Dr. No like in James Bond."

Bert looked at T and rolled her eyes. When prompted, she held out the splinted arm and let Dr. No carefully remove its encasement. The skin was crisscrossed with red lines, puffy and purple in a few places, nearly white in others. The kid winced. So did T. Bert simply looked at it.

"That looks like a bad one," Dr. No said.

"It's the only one I've had," Bert said. "But it's bad enough."

"Let's get it into a cast today. I guarantee it'll feel better when it doesn't get jostled around as much."

Dr. No turned to the sink and began preparing a cast. He pulled out rolls of gauze and cotton and a woven sleeve, wrapped and wrapped

Bert's arm, squeezed gently, apologized when Bert winced, snipped and inspected, and finally sat back.

"You're all set!" he said, then winked. "That's a cast joke. Because the plaster is set."

"Don't quit your day job," Bert said.

Dr. No laughed again and swept the crumpled wrappers and leftover gauze into the trash. He snapped off the gloves he'd been wearing and dropped them in too.

"Well, if you want better jokes, you've got to go somewhere fancier than this place," he said. "I hear they're pretty good at Mayo, but knock wood you don't go there, okay?"

Bert looked at him stony-faced, but T could see a little glint of amusement in her eyes. Dr. No was unbreakable, relentlessly cheery, and pretty much not so bad, especially when he carefully helped Bert slip off the exam table to the ground and stood with arms out to catch her if she lost her balance while getting her sea legs.

"Get back, you!" she said, but there wasn't much heat in it. "I'm not frail!"

"I can see that," Dr. No said. "Good thing. Keep up whatever you're doing and you'll heal up quick!"

With that, he was off. The curtains whipped closed behind him, and, frowning, Bert looked at her newly secured wrist. "This thing is giant," she said. "I guarantee it won't fit through my coat sleeve."

She was right, and they had to rig another wraparound, belt-it-up situation just to get her home. T worried about getting her dress off later but figured Bert wouldn't allow access to such a private moment anyway. *Digging her own grave,* T thought. Help *helped.* But Bert didn't usually permit help, especially if it involved the indignity of nudity.

IT TURNED OUT BERT DID get stuck in her dress and, after much argument, they decided to cut very carefully through the sleeve seam just enough to let her escape. T assured her that only the seam's threads, not fabric, would be cut, so that it could be mended later. Still, Bert was furious at the decision, even if it was the only one possible to make and was definitely not T's fault.

T helped Bert wrap herself in her bathrobe and then settled her into her bed with a glass of water, a pill and a book—Allende, *The House of the Spirits,* which T had found just a week ago, fanned out and abandoned in the laundromat.

Once Bert was snugged in and quietly reading, T set out on a mission: two buses and a four-block walk to the Goodwill, but it was worth it. T found a modest, pale yellow sleeveless dress and a cardigan loose enough to stretch over Bert's cast and then shuttled them back home to surprise her. T was pretty confident Bert would be much happier in the full coverage of completely intact clothing.

Bert was sleeping, and the book had fallen to the floor next to the bed, so T laid the dress and cardigan across the foot of the bed like a present and went to enjoy the luxury of cooking a hot meal on a working stove. The privilege never seemed to get old.

CHAPTER 12

RICHES

IN THE MORNING, T CHECKED on Bert before she stirred. Mouth open, head flopped to the side, casted arm flung onto the pillow above her head, she looked like a murdered starlet gone gray, though T tried not to think that and refreshed the glass of water at her bedside, left two Tylenol beside the water and scribbled a note. Once Bert had been squared away for the day, T hurried the few blocks to the bus stop to get to the laundromat.

Three of the eight washing machines were broken and the TV appeared to be on the fritz, so the laundromat seemed quieter than usual, though T had to field at least a dozen complaints from irritated launderers. It was probably telling that more people complained about the TV than the washers. A few of them, T suspected, came to the laundromat solely to watch *The Price Is Right* on the fuzzy, ancient screen. The TV had a looping wire antenna that occasionally had to be adjusted and a big metal dial like a cartoon TV. In order to change the channel or turn it on or off, T had to stand on a chair to reach the dial. They probably didn't even make remotes when that TV was made.

The air was overheated and heavy with the perfume of detergent, and around twelve T started to drowse. It was normally hard to do, but the place was quieter without the blinging babble of the TV and with so few patrons. Just as T's head began to drop slowly toward the desktop, a napkin-wrapped chocolate doughnut appeared there. T jerked back and looked up. Kohl leaned over the counter, beaming.

"Hi, Sugar Cookie! Got a seat for the bearer of coffee and dough-nuts?" She wiggled a paper bag that seemed to be heavy with coffee cups.

"Kohl! You're alive!" T gestured her to get behind the counter and grab her usual chair.

"Of course I'm alive," she snorted, coming through the half-door and flinging herself into the chair. "I thought you mastered object constancy as a baby."

"Peekaboo," T said sheepishly, and smooched her on the cheek. She smelled clean, like flowers and mint. Her hair was pulled tightly into a giant bun that was so big it looked as if it might topple her head. The bald sides were growing in but still pretty short, so she looked a little like a twelve-year-old boy with a giant topknot. Wisps of hair had slithered out and hung in coils at her cheeks. She wore a pink sweater and fresh-looking blue jeans; cowboy boots had replaced the spreading gold ballerina flats she used to wear. She even had a dainty gold necklace with a fierce red stone glistening at her throat. She looked and smelled like money. Like comfort.

"I miss you," she said simply and wrinkled her forehead. "You look skinny."

"You got plump," T said. "It hasn't even been that long."

"Thanks a lot," she snipped.

"No, I mean pleasantly. You look healthy, like you're eating real food."

"Uh huh," Kohl said. She seemed unconvinced. Looking as defiant as she could, she rummaged in the bag and pulled out a second doughnut for herself and shoved a good portion of it into her mouth.

T scraped a little icing off the doughnut, licked it off a finger, and said, "I'm not winning this, am I?"

"Not likely," Kohl said around her own doughnut.

"Then we're changing the subject. How's The Stupendous Kevin?"

"I'm sure he's still stupendously boring, just like he was when I left him." Kohl sniffed and used a pen to poke some of the stray tendrils of hair back into the bun on her head. Without the yammering TV, it was spooky-quiet, and the hum of the machines seemed louder than it should have, as if they were closing in. Kohl looked at T as though she wanted a fight.

Several questions fought their way to T's mouth, and everything seemed to come out at once. "You did what? I'm so... Where are you now?"

Kohl smirked. "It's okay. I know you didn't like the guy, and you were probably right. Just, what a jerk, I mean. He acted like he owned me. Plus, I couldn't take the humiliation and the sequins anymore. I'm still picking sequins out of my hair, and it's been days."

"It was a very sparkly outfit," T said.

"The glitter confetti was worse. That got everywhere." Kohl raised her eyebrows in a significant look when she said that, and T figured she meant the glitter had worked its way into her...crevices.

"Where are you now, then?"

"I've been bunking with Twee, actually."

"You can't stand her!"

"She's not that bad, once you get used to all the constant movement." Kohl tipped back and forth, pretending to dance in her seat. "Sometimes I still need to take a Dramamine to be around her, though."

"Can I have my quarters back? The washer stopped working. Again." Leaning over the counter was a woman buttoned tightly into a denim shirtwaist dress. She poked the countertop with her finger. "There's, like, one washer working now. My clothes are completely soaking. I have to take them somewhere else. Can I at least have my quarters back?"

T winced, tried to look apologetic, and slid a stack of quarters in her direction. "Sorry, so sorry. I've already contacted the owner about the washers."

"I should hope so," she said. The overworked buttons on her dress looked ready to give. "Thanks." She scooped the quarters into her palm and turned to go. After glopping her wet laundry into one of the plastic carts, she turned back. "Do you happen to have a plastic bag for this mess?"

Kohl hopped up, grabbed a plastic garbage bag, and passed it to the woman.

"Thanks a million," the woman said and dumped the laundry into the bag. She stabbed her way into a denim jacket, hoisted the bag of clothes (still dripping through some unseen hole in the plastic) onto her shoulder, and flounced out of the laundromat. They watched her push out of the door and onto the street; a dark water stain crept down the back of the jacket as she went.

"He tried to give me fifty bucks before I left, like I'm some sort of prostitute," Kohl said.

"Did you take it?"

"No way. But I took a good long shower before going. Plus I took the bottle of shampoo."

T opened the bag of coffee and pulled out the cups that had been neglected in Kohl's rush for the doughnuts. The bottom of the bag was full of sugar packets. Kohl took the second cup of coffee for herself, then grabbed the napkins and sugar packets and shoved them into her pocket. "For later," she said.

Kohl told T that she and Twee were staying at the shelter again, the one at which Twee had stayed before, and being there together was much less scary and not so bad.

"It's just until we figure out a place to be," Kohl said.

"I'd never in a million years imagine you staying with Twee willingly."

"We've come to an agreement," Kohl shrugged. "It's symbiotic."

"Tell her I have her cage," T said, gesturing to the dog cage at the side of the room. Kohl looked at it, at the lump of blankets inside, and frowned.

"I don't think she needs it anymore. She's eating. She's moved on to other projects." Kohl put her hand on T's cheek, suddenly weirdly fond. "You okay? Where are you?"

T tried hard not to jerk away from Kohl's touch but managed only to take the violence out of the move. "I'm with the P.O.L., actually."

"What?" Kohl exclaimed. She leaned toward T, eyes bright. The laundromat was so quiet, it sounded as if Kohl had screamed, but it had probably been closer to a loud whisper. "The P.O.L.? She's not a ghost?"

"Hardly," T said. "She's crackers. But lovely. And kindly giving me a place to stay."

"I went by the squat but I saw it was locked up. I got worried for you."

"Bert—the P.O.L.—she's great. I think my crush is even bigger than when she used to come into the laundromat."

Kohl batted her eyes and looked dramatically dreamy. "So dignified. So mysterious."

"So amazing. You have to talk to her sometime. She tells good stories. Come to visit!" T thought better of it. "But it'll have to wait. She's got a broken wrist right now and is pretty out of it."

After what seemed like only five minutes but was probably closer to half an hour, Kohl said she needed "to get back," though she didn't specify to what. T didn't ask, but Kohl said she'd be back to the laundromat the next day and she could stay longer so they could talk. She smacked a kiss on T's forehead, then scrubbed at the spot with her thumb.

"Sorry," she said when T flinched. "Lipstick." With that and a wave, she wafted out.

T WASN'T SURE WHETHER OR not to tell Bert about running into Kohl, but it quickly became irrelevant. When T got to Bert's, she was sleeping, though it looked as though she'd been up and about for some part of the day. Tea was spilled all over the kitchen table, one of the cups was overturned and a few cloth napkins had been piled into the mess in a poor attempt to sop it up.

T wiped everything dry, then snuck to Bert's room to find her nestled into the pillows and blankets of her bed. T refilled the water glass from the bathroom sink, adjusted Bert's blankets, and left the room.

Not a minute later, Bert hollered weakly, "T? Are you back?"

"It's me," T called, hustling again toward Bert's room. "You okay?"

Bert had propped herself up and pulled her robe tightly across her chest. Her cheeks had a healthy pink flush for the first time since the accident. She smoothed her hair. "I must look like a big mess," she said.

"Actually, I was just thinking how much better you look today. Feeling better?"

"Much, actually. I don't think I can sleep anymore or stay in this bed for one more minute, though."

T helped Bert to the kitchen and threw together some weak-tasting soup that Bert wouldn't swallow until T fixed it with a little tomato paste and salt. Afterward, T made a fresh pot of tea and peeled a tangerine for them to share. Bert instructed T where to find a board for checkers, and they played and drank tea and ate tangerine sections for most of a very pleasant evening.

"Thank you so much for that beautiful dress," Bert said. "You know my taste very well."

"I know how big your wrist is right now," T responded.

"Let me pay you for what you spent."

T squinted at her. "It's a gift, Bert. Just take it. I've managed to save up a little money from the laundromat."

Bert squinted back and waved her hand. "I can manage it just fine, and you need to be saving your money. You're not going to live with me forever, I expect."

T's heart bumped, thinking of Kohl, then thinking of the P.O.L. alone in her Proper Old House drinking tea from her Proper Old Teacup at the kitchen table. Bert looked at T and frowned.

"Of course, you can stay here as long as you'd like. But I imagine you don't want to live with an old lady like me." Her fingers crawled over the cotton tablecloth. She actually looked nervous.

"Bert, you're being ridiculous. I love being here. Plus, you're not an old lady."

"I think we've already established that I am," Bert said.

"What I mean is, you might be... in your sixties—"

"Thank you," Bert said. She patted T's arm.

"—but you're definitely not an *old lady*. You don't act like an *old lady*. That's just a state of mind, like you've just given everything up. You haven't. You're definitely not an *old lady*."

"Well," Bert said. "I think that's a compliment. I'm going to take it as a compliment, anyway." She took a long sip from her tea and stared at the calendar hanging above the table on the yellow wall. It was dusty, and two years too old, and open to April, but it featured a picture of lily of the valley flowers smattered with drops of rain. Bert probably kept it for the picture.

"Tomorrow, I'm getting dressed and spending the day awake," Bert said.

As she'd promised, in the morning, T found Bert already awake, sipping tea at the kitchen table and wearing the sunny yellow dress and the cardigan buttoned all the way up. When T came in, Bert had just taken a sip, but she gestured to the dress and beamed.

She swallowed the mouthful of tea. "It's just beautiful! Thank you again!"

"And it all fit over your cast!"

Bert looked pleased.

"Unbutton the cardigan, though, so we can see the dress better." T began to reach toward Bert to help her, but Bert's hands flew to cover the buttons at her chest, and she shook her head. T figured she was without a bra—doing the hooks one-handed was probably still too tall an order for Bert. T backed away with an apology.

"Chilly, huh?"

"Yes," Bert said, and took a long sip of her tea. They both knew Bert wasn't chilly at all and they both knew that they both knew. T silently agreed not to broach the subject again. Bert looked relieved.

She seemed to be so much better that morning. Something released inside T's chest, some knot that had probably been there for days. Bert had even attempted a little makeup, though she'd not tried the eyeliner or eyebrows—those probably required too much precision for her at the moment. But she'd powdered her face, scrubbed on a little rouge, even pulled her hair back into an orange flowered scarf.

"Now that you're up and about, I feel bad leaving you for the day, but I have to go to work," T said.

Bert waved at an invisible fly. "No bother! I have a good book and a new dress and a pot of tea. I'm very happy right here."

KOHL BREEZED INTO THE LAUNDROMAT just before noon carrying hot noodles and vegetables from the Chinese takeout next door.

"Lunch!" she called, wiggling the bag in the air.

It smelled wonderful, hot, a little spicy, more substantial than what T was used to eating, even with Bert. T and Kohl sat and ate noisily. Outside the office window, nearly nobody was washing laundry. It should have been busier, but the laundromat had been steadily losing patrons—as steadily as it had been growing dirtier and more broken-down. It was hard to tell which was the initial problem, the broken chicken or the sparse eggs.

While they ate, Kohl told T she had a job as a secretary in her old departmental office at Pitt so she could go back to school again. Trouble was, though, that it was hard to take classes because she was working most of the time. She had a crazy schedule on weekdays, and weekends were mostly spent at the library trying to get work done.

When she wasn't doing either of those things, she was working with Twee on what they were calling The Sanitary Project. The name had been Twee's idea, and Kohl thought it was pretty awful, but she just didn't have the energy to come up with anything better. It didn't matter anyway—it wasn't as though anyone ever needed to know the name of the project. It was highly unofficial, and the point was to accomplish a good thing, not to make a name for themselves. They were stealing toilet paper and menstrual pads and distributing them among the homeless folks they could find on the street. It was an idea they'd been kicking around for a while, but they had only just started making the rounds on a regular basis.

It was perfect, T thought: just the right amount of theatrical grand gesture for Kohl and the exact balance of poorly planned-but-well-meaning action that seemed to attract Twee.

"The name's pretty terrible, though," T ventured.

"I know. It sounds vaguely fascist."

T grunted; that was about right. Fascism always seemed just one step beyond impulsive idealism anyway. The same kind of unconsidered devotion to a purpose seemed to drive it.

"Still," Kohl said. "I feel like we're actually making a difference this time. It's good."

"It's very Robin Hood, but with toilet paper," T said.

Kohl rolled her eyes. "Don't joke. It's pretty important. Nobody thinks about those little things until they can't get them. Then those little things mean everything."

"Preaching to the choir, Kohl," T said, trying to keep a nasty edge from curling over the words. Maybe Kohl had forgotten exactly what it was like living the way they had in the squat. Clearly, things had gotten pretty comfortable for her.

"I know what you're thinking. It isn't true," Kohl said. "I'm living at a shelter, for god's sake. I've got a tiny, squeaky little girl as a bodyguard. I am definitely still in touch with reality."

T mashed the remaining crumbs of doughnut into a blob, then rolled the blob into a solid ball and ate it. It was a disgusting habit, T knew, and Kohl made a face.

"Still with that?" she said.

T gave Kohl an irritated look and beamed a silent *Oh, please* at her.

"We're looking for a way to get out of the shelter, you know," Kohl said. "I can't take it anymore. We're trying to find a place."

"A new squat?"

Kohl took a long gulp of coffee. "I guess. I'm pretty sick of squatting, but rent is steep, even with the two of us. Twee thinks she found a place, a house we can easily break into in Oakland. It's even got a few pieces of furniture left in there. Who knows how long it'll stay empty, but we might try it."

T didn't respond—it sounded nicer than the old squat, at least. A house had rooms with doors, usually; they probably wouldn't even need the blanket-tents. Kohl and T sat together, not speaking, and when the silence got too hard to bear, they drank coffee to avoid having to talk. At least, T was doing that, and was pretty sure Kohl was doing that too. Even after T ran out of coffee and the paper cup was empty, T continued to pretend to sip, raising the empty cup and faking a swallowing motion, just to avoid speaking. The whole situation felt a little dangerous—rather tenuous, with too many things unsaid and threatening to topple over them.

"You could come live with us again," Kohl said. "We could find a place that's good for all of us, if you want."

Her voice sounded just as wobbly as the moment felt. Having roommates again sounded nice, but things weren't the same, and Kohl probably knew it.

Her coffee was gone, and she tossed the empty cup in the bin. T had been pretending to sip for far too long, and knew it wouldn't fly anymore either, so T faked one last sip, then tossed the cup in the bin after Kohl's.

"I don't think I can," T said, and heard Kohl's breath rush out in a sigh that could have been either disappointment or relief. "I'm going to stick close to Bert. She needs me to help her out right now."

Kohl crinkled her nose. "Pretty good setup you've got there."

There was no tone in her voice. T couldn't hear anything—not jealousy, not sympathy, not snark—and it was hard to tell how she meant it.

"You should talk, Mrs. Stupendous."

"I left that. I'm at a shelter. What do you want from me?" Kohl's voice was a needle point. T tried to push back from the counter, but the chair wheel got caught in a rut in the linoleum floor and wouldn't move. T felt stuck, and Kohl wouldn't stop staring, waiting.

The front door flumped closed, and T looked: Suddenly, there was nobody left in the laundromat except the two of them. Dust motes drifted in the weak sunlight by the entrance. The place looked haunted, empty, with that feeling that it had just been full and everyone had fled in a frantic rush. Without the machines running, it felt as if someone had cut off T's hearing. There was, suddenly, absolutely nothing.

Kohl rapped a knuckle on the counter. "Hello?" she said, leaning into T's eyeline.

"Yeah, sorry, I got lost," T said. "Sorry. You're right. I'm being awful."

"No, baby." Kohl twisted her hand into T's hair. "You're okay. You're under pressure right now, I bet."

Clearly, then, Kohl remembered the impending trial. T felt a little better about that—she hadn't forgotten her friends after all.

It just felt as if she had.

WHEN T GOT BACK TO Bert's house, Bert was sleeping again. This time, it looked like an unintended nap: Bert was sprawled out on the couch in the lovely yellow dress; the throw T used as a blanket was pulled over her hips, and her head sagged back onto the cushions.

T tiptoed around, gathering up her teacup, her cast-off cardigan, the notebook in which she'd apparently been writing. The kitchen, again, was a mess, with slopped tea on the counter and sugar spilled all around its bowl. The handle of the refrigerator had pulled loose and was hanging crooked by one screw. Bert had gotten so sloppy in her recovery. T figured it was the pain or the Tylenol putting her off her game. T tidied up while Bert slept.

Bert clearly needed more help during the day, and T was never around.

T crept to the basement to look for something to fix the refrigerator handle. There had to be a container of screws and a screwdriver, or at least some wire or tape for a quick, temporary fix. How the P.O.L. ever made it down those stairs, T would never know. Old wood, rickety, pocked with splinters and jutting nails, the staircase seemed like a deathtrap. T went down slowly with one hand braced on the wall.

The basement mimicked the shape of the house above it and was even divided into a facsimile of the rooms on the first floor. Light seeped through tiny casement windows near the ceiling; the cement floor bubbled up in places, making molehills of rubble and dirt. T searched the space under the stairs and then the one under the living room, but found nothing save a few moldering carboard boxes. Pulling the lid back on the top one in the stack revealed carefully folded sweaters and dresses and several pairs of shoes, all precisely stored. The shoes were each wrapped in a paper towel. The clothing was folded around tissue paper, probably to keep wrinkles at bay. It smelled musty, but everything looked pristine.

T thought about pulling some of it out of storage and encouraging Bert to wear it. There was so much there, and it was all in good shape, and she seemed to have so little otherwise. T resisted and carefully refolded the box top. There was probably a good reason Bert had stored it.

But when T turned on the overhead bulb in the next room, the one under the kitchen, the light felt like a slap. Against the wall directly below the kitchen sink was a washer and dryer set.

T stood for a long time in the dim basement room, just looking at the machines. They were plugged into an outlet halfway up the wall. They gleamed clean and white and looked barely used, almost new. The washer still had a bright yellow paper instructional tag glued to the top.

"I've been washing your clothes at the laundromat," T said to nobody. The machines sat silently, squat and fat, gleaming in a sort of mean smirk.

WHEN T WENT BACK UPSTAIRS, the clomp of the basement door closing startled Bert awake on the couch. Lost somewhere between sleeping and waking, she stared at T without seeing. She looked wild in the low afternoon light. Wisps of sweaty hair stuck to her cheeks.

"I'm up," Bert said. "What do you need?"

"I was just looking for something to fix the fridge handle. Do you have a screwdriver?"

"That damn piece of junk keeps falling off. I glued it before, but I don't think it stuck right. It came off again today."

"I can fix it if you have a screwdriver," T said. "I was looking in the basement but didn't find anything." T tried to inflect the words with extra significance, but Bert didn't seem to pick up on anything at all. She simply shook her head and rubbed at a crease the couch cushion had left on her neck.

"No tools, kiddo. Sorry."

"I looked all over the basement," T said again, but Bert still didn't notice.

"I'll give you money for the hardware store," she said. She took a checkbook out of the hulking black purse that sat on the coffee table and began to write. "I'm leaving the amount blank, so you can just fill it in when you go to the store."

She handed T the check. Her signature was large and unnecessarily looped, completely not what T might imagine it would look like. T tucked the check in a pocket.

"I can't go right away. I've got work."

"No bother," Bert said. "It can wait."

Still furious, T wanted to be rude, to grunt at Bert and storm out or perhaps make some other grand gesture of irritation. But Bert could melt anyone: the papery skin, the softening eyes, the halo of gray hair, it all made her look kind and harmless. She *was*; she *was* kind and harmless. She'd probably forgotten about the washer and dryer years ago. Or maybe she just went to the laundromat to be around other people. She led a pretty lonely life.

T would forgive her and T would fix the refrigerator handle and T would probably wash her dresses and cardigans at the laundromat again.

And T would never ask her about the machines in the basement, or the boxes full of clothes, or how much money she kept in that checking account, or what Telly had meant to Bert. The P.O.L. could have her secrets and she could keep that little inch of distance from T. T could live with her and love her and take care of her without being privy to everything. They didn't have to be exactly in sync. That was perfectly normal.

The thoughts ground inside T's chest like sharpened stones.

WHEN THE TIME CAME, KOHL and Twee met T at the bus stop near Bert's house and they took the bus to the courthouse together. T was wearing a pair of pants and a button-down shirt Bert had purchased from the Goodwill. The pants were slightly too tight; the shirt was slightly too baggy. Bert had shrugged and said wearing ill-fitting clothes might help T look more sympathetic. When she'd offered to come along, T had refused her—it didn't seem at all kind to drag her out in the heat for something in which she'd had no part. It would probably be quick anyway—T was simply going to stand up in front of the judge, and the judge would decide what would happen to T, and then T would have to deal with the consequences, alone, yet another time. T had discovered that that was how the world was. The lawyer had said that the whole thing would probably take less than fifteen minutes once T got up in front of the judge. It was the waiting around that took all the time.

"Thanks, but it's really no big deal," T had said to Bert.

The P.O.L. had looked sad when she said, "It is. A big deal, it is. It's your future."

"WE'VE MISSED YOU," KOHL SAID (again) as they stepped off the bus. T nodded and wondered exactly when Kohl had begun including Twee in her "we."

"You have to come visit the new place," Twee said. "It's got rooms, even."

"There's always a room for you, if you want it," Kohl said quietly.

Twee and Kohl were stationed on either side of T with their arms wrapped around T so tightly it was hard to walk. It was only a couple blocks, but the sun was pummeling them, and T felt sweaty and uncomfortable, the way they pressed and clung. T tried to twist, politely, out of their grip in order to walk a little more freely, but Twee only gripped tighter.

"Almost lost you, you slippery devil!" she said. "Got you now."

With a jerk, Kohl stopped walking. She was staring across the street. T stopped, too, which yanked Twee backwards.

"Is that..." Twee started.

"Vas. It's Vas," Kohl said.

They all watched as Vas left the office supply store. He was wearing khaki pants and a white shirt with a red nametag pinned crookedly to the chest. He crossed the street and seemed to be walking right toward them without seeing them at all.

"Come on," T said and pulled Twee and Kohl forward. What was coming was inevitable, and T just wanted to get it over with. They didn't have time for a screaming match with Vas—T had to get to the courthouse.

Vas was looking at his chest and adjusting his nametag pin when their paths met. He didn't even see them.

"Vas," Kohl said. He looked up.

"Hi," she said.

Vas looked as though he might stop, but he didn't. He smoothed the front of his white shirt, nodded at them, and kept going. Kohl's jaw dropped.

"Did you—" she started.

"Doesn't matter," T said. "Just let him go."

Kohl huffed, so T squeezed her arm and said, "I'll meet you after."

"You don't want us to come?" Twee said. "We should come."

"There's nothing for you to do. I just have to go in and get it over with."

They'd reached the stoplight at the corner and had to stand waiting while traffic inched past. Everything seemed to move slowly in the heat. The city smelled that damp summer smell of sewage and steam and closeness. Behind them, Vas turned the corner and walked up the ramp of Three Rivers Parking.

"Okay," Kohl said. "We'll meet you later. I'm going to go to the library. I'll be back here at four." She pecked T on the cheek and turned back to head for the bus stop. T and Twee watched her lope up the hill and out of sight with her satchel bouncing against her hip. As she jogged, she twisted her hair into a knot on the top of her head and stabbed a pen through it to keep it in place.

"I'm going to go to the river just to walk around," Twee said. "Unless you want company. I don't mind waiting there somewhere if you don't want me to be in the actual courtroom."

It was the most sedate T had ever seen her. She'd made an effort to dress for court, too, that much was clear. She wore a blue cotton dress that reached well past her knees. The dress was sleeveless, but it was fitted and sober-looking and probably the best she could find at the thrift store. She crooked a small half-smile. "I really don't mind. There's probably air conditioning."

"No, no. Thanks, though," T said. "I'm fine."

"Are you really?" Twee said. Her face was full of such sympathy. Her brows were drawn together, and her eyes looked watery. She bit her lip.

"Everything's good," T said. "Go enjoy the breeze at the river."

Twee turned to go. She was red-faced, holding-in, small. T felt sorry for her and waved before turning toward the courthouse.

"If you're sure you're okay," she called as she left.

The Allegheny courthouse looked more like a flattened castle than a modern building: gray stone and arched windows and peaked gray roof. T could see it down the street in the middle of the block. It was heavy enough that the road seemed to bend slightly under its weight. Too much stone.

"I'm okay," T said, though not loudly enough to reach Twee as she disappeared up the block. It was more of a thought, an under-the-breath thought. *I'm going to be okay.*

CHAPTER 13

BEFORE AND AFTER

T MET WITH THE LAWYER briefly, then waited in a small under-ventilated room, adjusted and readjusted the pants and shirt, wiped the sweat that seemed to trickle from everywhere, tried to breathe evenly in the heat.

Finally, someone came to escort T to the large desk at the front of the room which faced the judge's even larger desk. The judge sat, they stood, then they sat, then the judge shuffled papers. Everything seemed to slide by without sticking—no moment slowed enough to make sense, and the whole room seemed to be slipping sideways.

"You okay?" the lawyer said. She was kind but still businesslike, and so T nodded and didn't explain that the place was tipping drastically like a sinking ship.

"You look a little green." She pushed a cup of water in T's direction. T nodded and drank while the judge shuffled and shuffled the papers and did not look up.

Then there was a hand on T's shoulder.

T turned. It was Kohl, who smiled weakly and shrugged. "Drink it," she said and poked.

T drank again and swallowed.

"I got halfway to the bus stop and turned around," Kohl said. "Doesn't matter if you don't want me here, because here I am. And I found these two waiting in the back."

Next to Kohl was Twee. Twee sat carefully on the edge of her seat, looking earnestly serious, her arm draped protectively around the shoulders of the P.O.L. Bert looked stiff and uncomfortable. Her powdery skin was wet in the heat, like damp tissue. She wore the yellow dress; her hair was carefully pinned into a knot at the back of her head. T had no idea how she'd managed that so neatly with the cast, but not a hair strayed out of place.

Bert shrugged out from under Twee's arm and patted T's shoulder. "It didn't feel right, sitting at home while you were here, facing down your future," she said.

"Thank you," T said and meant it.

The P.O.L. smiled reassuringly. "I want to be here for your future."

Twee nodded and nodded. She was sniffling, and T was thankful she didn't try to talk, lest it come out in an inappropriately loud wail. Instead, she thrust a wilting handful of clover flowers in T's direction.

"This feels a little After School Special," T said.

Kohl laughed. "Don't be an ass. Just accept it. You've got a crew."

The judge cleared her throat and flipped the manila folder closed.

"We got you," Kohl whispered. She squeezed T's shoulder and sat back.

"All right," the judge said. "Mr. Persaud?"

T sighed because *this* was how it was going to go. Once again.

The lawyer jerked her chair back, pulling T to stand next to her. T stood on shaky legs. There were no windows. The room was small and ugly, over-weighted with dark wood. A flag hung limp behind the judge. If there had been a blackboard, it would have looked exactly like public school.

There was scraping, shifting, clearing of throats; the smattering of people sitting in the benches behind T shuffled and hacked.

T reached one hand back to grip the top of the chair so as not to fall over. It was too hot, too close in the room, full of sweat and anxious bodies and echo. The P.O.L. wrapped her hand around T's wrist.

"We're right behind you," she whispered.

ACKNOWLEDGMENTS

I'D LIKE TO EXTEND OFFICIAL thanks to everyone who helped me along the way with this novel. Several people helped improve the representation of Trini, Indian-American, Asian-American, and immigrant cultures; others helped with the representation of transgender/nonbinary/gender nonconforming experience; still others gave advice as medical professionals and psychotherapists who work with TGNCNB and immigrant clients. This novel has been in many hands, but I'd especially like to thank Dr. Kori Bennet; Irina Fabre, N.P.; Dr. Kit Rachlin; Joy Huang Clark; and Dr. Sonya Vieira for their loving and dedicated help. I'd also like to thank, once again, Annie Harper, who is perhaps the keenest and most supportive editor in the world, and Morgan Morrison, who helped me get the thing out and tell people about it. Mostly, this book would not have come to be without the advice, encouragement, and sharp intelligence of my writing/editing partner Laura Stone, who is a friend and novelist I deeply admire.

I owe one of the biggest debts to my partner, Dr. B. Donatone, who advised from both personal and professional perspectives, supported me without fail, and knows exactly when to push and when to distract me. And sometimes shows up with cupcakes at the right moment. You, my love, are my favorite. Thank you.

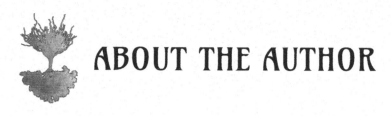# ABOUT THE AUTHOR

ALYSIA CONSTANTINE IS A CRITICALLY acclaimed and award-winning author whose novels blur the line between reality and fantasy, feature luscious prose and explore complex themes of otherness. Her novels *Sweet* (Interlude Press, 2016) and *Olympia Knife* (Interlude Press, 2017) received starred reviews from *Publishers Weekly* and *Foreword Reviews*, respectively. She is also the editor of the 2020 Young Adult anthology, *Short Stuff* (Duet Books). She lives in the Lower Hudson Valley with her wife, two dogs, and a cat and is a former professor at a New York arts college.

interlude**press**™

🌐 interludepress.com
🐦 @InterludePress
📘 interludepress
🛒 store.interludepress.com

interlude  press
also by Alysia Constantine

Olympia Knife
Foreword Reviews Starred Review recipient

Born into a family of trapeze artists, Olympia Knife leads an idyllic life as a travelling circus performer until her fellow troupers vanish before her eyes. First are Olympia's parents, the Flying Knives, who disappear midair during their act. Second is Arnold, The World's Smallest Major General (he was neither) Tiny Napoleon Only Three Feet Tall, followed by Magnus, the lobster-clawed circus director—one by one, they are all, simply, gone. Into the fray walks Diamond the Danger Eater, daring and determined, and together she and Olympia face their crumbling world, having only each other to cling to in the struggle for existence.

In the tradition of magical realism, *Olympia Knife* is a tale of survival and resistance for LGBTQ folks and all others who live unseen, untethered, or outside the margins.

ISBN (print) 978-1-945053-27-6 | (eBook) 978-1-945053-44-3

Sweet
Publishers Weekly Starred Review recipient

Jules Burns is a lonely baker mourning the loss of his husband, Andy. Teddy Flores is a numbed-to-the-world accountant who accidentally stumbles into his bakery and, with the help of a mouthy baker's assistant, some good pastry and Jules himself, rediscovers his deep connections to pleasure, to the world and to his own heart.

Sweet is also the story of how we tell stories—of what we expect and need from a love story. The narrator is on to you, Reader, and wants to give you a love story that doesn't always fit the bill. There are ghosts to exorcise, and jobs and money to worry about. Sweet is a love story, yes, but a story that reminds us that love is never quite what we expect, nor quite as blissfully easy as we hope.

ISBN (print) 978-1-941530-61-0 | (eBook) 978-1-941530-62-7